S0-DTD-596

A
PERFECT STRANGER

FIRTH HARING

SIMON AND SCHUSTER · NEW YORK

Copyright © 1973 by Firth Haring
All rights reserved
including the right of reproduction
in whole or in part in any form
Published by Simon and Schuster
Rockefeller Center, 630 Fifth Avenue
New York, New York 10020

First printing

SBN 671-21470-5
Library of Congress Catalog Card Number: 72-90394
Designed by Eve Metz
Manufactured in the United States of America

FOR CARL, WITH LOVE

1

AT my thirty-fourth birthday party, I feel even more like a child than usual. My mother and father are here, my aunt and uncle are here, my best friend, Connie, is here, and my children, my benign smiling husband, and my three-layer cake with candles and pink sugar roses are here. And when they have sung Happy Birthday and I have blown out the candles, everyone who is here clamors to know what I have wished for. "A happy life," I say.

"*That* wish has already come true," says my mother, triumphantly. As if it were her doing.

"You couldn't ask for anything more," says my aunt.

"A happy life," announces my husband. "Right, Connie?"

"Yeah," says Connie, holding out her wine glass for more. "She's got it made."

"You're all so smart," I say, handing the cake around.

At the end of the evening as I am helping my mother on with her coat, she says, in the dim light of the front hall, "A man doesn't have to put up with that kind of ingratitude. Just remember where you came from, my girl."

I move the coat away from her a little, so she has to stretch to get her arthritic arm into it. She looks at me, craning her neck around like a wounded turtle, to see if I have done it on purpose.

And after they have all piled into the cars and driven away in the dark with loud cries of Happy Birthday ringing through the trees, Jonas asks, "Is it the family that got to you, or just another birthday?"

"It's my life," I say dully, scraping ice cream and cake into the garbage pail. "My boring, unproductive, empty, and ridiculous life."

He carries coffee cups and wine glasses in from the dining room and stacks them in the dishwasher. He empties ash trays. "We've been through all this before," he says.

I rinse the cake plates and forks. "Yes. I'm sorry it keeps cropping up."

He wipes off the table and counters with a wet sponge. He is always quite a help to me around the house, when he's here. "Why don't you come to the meeting in Palm Beach with me?"

"A sop."

"Lily. I want you to be happy."

"Let me go back to work."

"Your place is with your children."

"My children don't need me." Don't you see that, you Victorian predator.

"They do need you. They're only five and three."

"They're almost six and three and a half." I follow him around the downstairs from room to room as he turns out lights, whistles for the cat, and checks the windows and doors. "They're in school all morning, Jonas. They nap in the afternoon. Then they're out playing. When do they need me? Tell me that. They need me to make three meals

8

a day and chauffeur them to school. Somebody else could do that."

"When they're older, Lily," he says, putting his arm around me as we start up the stairs to bed. "Hang on for a few more years. Come to the meeting in Palm Beach. You need a little rest."

And so that is how it started. We packed the boys off to their grandmother's for a week, and I went with Jonas to Palm Beach and was approached by Ian.

Jonas is the executive vice-president and marketing director of Fleming & Fleming, piano manufacturers. Among other things, it is his job to conduct a national sales meeting once a year designed to acquaint all the Fleming men in the field with the new pianos and organs that, come spring, they are to sell to all the retail music stores in America.

This year it is Jonas's special burden to tell them that Fleming has just had its worst year since the Depression. Nobody is buying pianos. He will comfort them with the news that the entire keyboard industry is suffering from rising costs and falling sales and that everyone is having a bad year. And then every day, numerous times a day, he will exhort them to get out there and show their stuff, to get those nifty new models into the showrooms, if they have to break their asses doing it.

The men love it, he tells me.

While all this is going on, I lie on the beach and forget about winter in Westchester. It was five degrees the day we left, and I was straining with passion to get away from it all. Do I sound like an unnatural mother? I am a Capricorn. We are devoted to our children.

January in Palm Beach is not January in the Virgin Islands, where we, Jonas and I alone, once spent a week, but it is a mild January in Florida this year, and though the Floridians don't dream of exposing themselves on the beach in January, I, sprung by 70 degrees from my winter wools, turn my body over to the sun every day in front of a tiny gay cabana I have rented for the week. I lie there. I read. I tan. I forget about home. I watch the ocean. I think it does not look much like the ocean we go to in the summer. It is smaller somehow, less wild. A tame, baylike, surfless ocean, good for children and bathing and finding shells, which on the crashing shores northward we hardly ever find whole.

I walk along the beach wearing my bright caftan, because vertically one feels the coolness in the January air more than horizontally on the baking sand in front of the cabana, where I lie without it, warm, and hopeful that Jonas will come and lie beside me.

I *wish* he would give them all some time off, so he could come and be with me and act as if it is a vacation we are having, instead of a bribe I am accepting. I wish he would do that.

On the third day, when I am lying alone on my private desert, Ian arises from the sea and lopes over to me. I put aside my book and draw the caftan over my bare brown legs.

"Hello!"

"Hello!"

I am glad for someone to talk to. "Cutting classes?"

"Yes! Deadly this year. Jonas is on our backs."

"Your hair!"

"Oh," he says. "In the South, the wilder I look, the more pianos I sell."

"It's unreal." The men in my world are all tonsured like cadets.

"What's real?" he asks, moving around me and my mat as if to view me from every angle. "The real should be the ideal, but it hardly ever is, is it?"

I look at him.

"Things are not always what they seem," he says. "Remember your Plato?"

I am not at home with philosophical conversations. Jonas and I are very down to earth, so I just shrug and examine a loose thread in my caftan. I would like to discourage him from going on in this heavy vein. After all, does it matter if hair in the general is independent of Ian's hair in the particular, or if hair has no existence of its own but is merely a generalization of Ian's hair? Not to me.

But, then, of course, it is not hair that he is talking about. He is saying that he is not what he appears to be, and perhaps that I am not what I appear to be. We appear to be . . . What *do* we appear to be?

"Don't mind me," he says, as if he senses that I am put off by philosophy. But I mind his roaming around me like some stag in estrus more than I do his trying to draw me into a discussion of the nature of reality. He senses that too. "I'll sit down as soon as my legs dry off," he says.

I squint up at him tall against the sun and smile at him. He is an ectomorph, like me. And fair, like me. I wonder what his sign is.

"I was a philosophy major in college," he says. "And a music minor. I taught music for a year to grade-school kids. Rhythm bands, triangles, tambourines, sticks, shakers. Wow. Nearly drove me out of my nut. I like peddling pianos better."

He seems so different today, so goofy, that I wonder if he has been drinking, or taking pep pills.

He arranges himself suddenly beside me in the sand,

11

alarming me with his bigness and near-nakedness so close. I do not know what to make of him. I never know what to make of people who play on words without indicating that they know they are.

"How has your year been?"

"Wild. They buy pianos like crazy in Savannah. I'm way up this year. Highest in the company. Everybody else is down."

"I know."

"Jonas tells you that sort of thing."

"Loves that company."

"Married to it?"

"You might say." I am put off again, offended that he should use my own metaphor for Jonas's career, and I turn away and gaze out at the water, sporting with white-caps.

"Listen, Lily," he says. "I'm sorry I said that. It was a stupid thing to say."

"Oh, that's all right," I say. "It doesn't bother me." I wish suddenly that my hair were as nice as his, as blond, as well cut. "How's Becky?"

"She's O.K. Going crazy with the kids."

Becky. Last year the company had a good year and paid for wives to go to the sales meeting in Miami. Becky was pregnant, and her maternity clothes were crusted with baby food from an earlier baby that she had fed in them while carrying her second. Her knees were oddly whiter than the rest of her legs, from what I had taken to be kneeling in puddles of Mr. Clean as she scrubbed floors, and there were hairs of an unidentifiable domestic animal on the seats of all her skirts. "What did she have?"

"Another girl. Three girls now. Do you mind if I lie down?"

With that wild hippie hair? With that big gangly body? "No," I say. "There's another mat in the cabana." Right in front of the hotel? Where they can all *see?*

I roll over onto my stomach while he hunts on his hands and knees inside my cabana for the mat. I am so glad now that I did not buy a bikini, as Jonas urged me to do. I regard my middle section as just as private as the parts that go under a bikini, and never let anyone see it, except Jonas, although it is worth seeing, flat and nice, except for a small mommy bulge under the navel, about the size of Jonas's hand.

We lie, then, on our fronts, heads on arms, observing each other with an eye apiece. I close mine now and then, believing that the eye is the mirror of the soul, and not wanting him to see my soul.

The sun beats down, stupefying me, relaxing me, carrying me into a mood realm of tropical languor and slackness. I don't care about anything I have left behind me. It is all forgotten in the sun.

This somnolence, this languor, this letting go makes me very sure I am hearing right when he says in a muffled voice, "I think about you." Somehow I know that. I know that there is something. That is why he is here.

"You think about me?" The sun is hotter today than it has been since we arrived, and I can feel it burning my back and the backs of my legs.

"All the time. Obsessed."

"Absurd. Ian. Please don't go on." Please do go on is what I mean. And he knows it, but he says that he is sorry, anyway, to play the game.

He is a marvel to me, a creature from another world. So different from Jonas, well-trimmed, well-groomed Jonas. I raise myself on my elbows to look at him. I make a furrow in the sand and play, letting little pinches of it fall between my fingers to fill the furrow, and then I make another furrow, and another. He is so still I think he has fallen asleep.

It is time for me to get going, but I find the temptation to stay too difficult to resist. "What is it that you think?" I ask after a long while. I am conscious of my aggression. I am doing this. Not he.

He props himself up on his elbow. "Do you really want to know?"

"Yes." Who wouldn't?

"Lily," he says, "you are my ideal woman. I worship you. I have for two years. I would like to become your Petrarchan lover and send you sonnets and play lays for you on my guitar, and kiss your hem, and swear undying fealty."

His conceit amazes me. It is far more elaborate and thought-out than I had expected. "Are you sure it's Petrarchan you mean, or are you working up to Launcelot?" See? I did it again.

"Petrarchan. Always. Never anything beyond."

I actually believe him, and find it not absurd at all. "Games people play."

"I know. Forget it. I'm a fool. You must despise me."

"I *am* happily married."

"I know. Of course. Jonas must be a wonderful husband. He's one of my heroes."

"He thinks very highly of you, too." I am so *prim!*

"If I could be half the man he is. He's fantastic. Keeps us all in line. What a leader." He rolls over in the sand and pulls the Tatami mat on top of him.

Jonas would never do what Ian is doing.

"I'm burning up," he says. "I'm burning up."

14

He is burning up for me is what he means. Oh, Lily. This is your time to get a move on. Instead I say, "Shall I cover your legs for you?" I throw my towel over his legs, which stick out from under the mat from the calves down. They are nice and straight and athletic and swirled with hair. "How old are you?" Not that that has anything to do with it. We are old enough to cut the mustard, as they say. "Twenty-eight. Do I seem like a callow ass to you? Forget what I said. I'll never bother you again."

"You're *not.*" Lily! I hold my destiny again, like a nut, in the cup of my hand. But I would *like* a neoplatonic lover. Who wouldn't?

"I've ruined my career. You'll tell Jonas. How could I be such a fool?"

"I'm not going to tell Jonas. I don't tell him everything. We're happily married and all that. Have our differences, of course. Doesn't every couple. But, we are happy. Really."

"I know. He's told me."

"He's told you about me?"

"Yes. Always. When he comes to Savannah. What a wonderful wife you are. His whole life."

"I'm not. I'm really not. I carp at him all the time. Nag him. Ungrateful. His job is so important. Takes him away so much. I'm alone."

His voice comes back strangled from under the mat: "That's what first attracted me. You seemed so alone. Secret."

It is inane, pointless, for me to go on lying here listening to a man say such things. But I want to. To tell him. "I feel very isolated," I say. "My boys are in school all morning. And our town is . . . woodsy. Lonely. Four-acre zoning and all that. I read a lot. Have a few friends. Get together with the mommies in the afternoons sometimes."

"I left Becky twice. Went back both times. Couldn't stand the guilt. Three kids to support now."

"You don't love her?"

"I do, I guess. Got married in college. She doesn't know what to make of me any more. I've changed; she hasn't. The old cliché. But I shouldn't talk about her. Out of respect. If we ever get out of debt. Just finished paying off my tuition loans. Went to composing school for a year after college. That set us back. Now the kids. What a life."

"No wonder you think about other women."

"Not other women. *You. Lily.* My ideal." All this from under the Tatami mat, which heaves and twists with his story.

I tell him again what he already knows—that we have been married for seven years, that we have two children, one in kindergarten, one in a Montessori nursery school. And then I tell him what he doesn't know—that sometimes I feel as if we have three. And that I'm the third. "The only difference is that they go to school, and I'm the dunce who stays home." I'm supposed to be the Boss's happy wife. I shouldn't say things like that.

He throws the mat off. "Does that mean I can write to you when the meeting is over?"

"No." Why should he think it would mean that?

"I'm sorry. I really won't mention it again." He lies down again in the sand and draws the mat back over him. "It's just that . . ."

"I know. Forget it. I'll just go on the way I was. Feed on you in my heart."

"*Stop* that! It makes me very sad. I like you." I plunge right in, knowing all the while that the little green hickory nut has the meat of my fate lying inside. But I'd like a neoplatonic lover. Who wouldn't? "Would I write back?"

He sits up, holding the mat around him like a prayer shawl. A calm comes into his eye. He knows he has me. "You could. It would be up to you."

"I'll see," I say, conscious that I am penetrating his eye with mine. He grabs my hand and kisses it, in full view of the windows where they are having their meetings. And then tall Ian with his fair hair flowing behind him lopes away in his cut-off jeans to hear my husband talk up the new pianos. He *appears* to be a young husband and father upward bound in his career.

2

LILY, my Laura, he writes in his first letter. If you could know what a relief it is to have you at last.

You mustn't talk about having me, I write to his post-office box. There won't be any such thing. We are to keep this in a sensible realm of pianos, books, and company politics. I am willing to listen only on those terms, being happily married.

I know you're happily married, he returns, the next day. Jonas is a prince. I know how happy you are. I don't want to hurt you. The last thing I want. We'll write only about books and pianos and how wonderful it would be if we could lie on the beach every day like that and talk and look into each other's eye and not have to go through a third party, the post office. Do you remember how it was the last night, when we danced and I had to put my hand on your bare back. It was so hot, from your sunburn. You have such a fine back.

Don't get carnal. It's Jonas's back. And dancing you must think of only as a symbol of concord and harmony, the formal union of two kindred souls. We are to elevate each other, and bare backs are not elevating. Let me put on Mrs. Borg's Swedish Meat Balls in Burgundy Sauce for the boys. I'll be right back.

Dearest Lily, he writes back. If you could know how my life is changed since Palm Beach. All my troubles seem to float away. I play to Becky every night on my guitar, and pretend she's you. It makes Becky so happy to be played to. See how *good* you make me. When will we meet again? Fifty more weeks till I hold you in my arms again. Couldn't you think up a reason for coming to Savannah? Separated by a thousand miles. Don't give your boys Mrs. Borg's Swedish Meatballs in Burgundy Sauce. It can kill them.

You're getting off the track. Got to stop writing stuff like that. Makes me nervous. Dancing with somebody isn't the same as holding them in your arms. I'm happily married. What if Jonas knew. He was here when the mailman came this morning. You must mail your letters so they don't arrive on Saturday. Is he planning a spring trip to Savannah? I can't ask. He might suspect. And why might Mrs. Borg's goodies be lethal?

Why should he suspect? Did he notice anything in Palm Beach? How about that day we were in the pool together? I sold three pianos for you this morning: three Mediterranean verticals to a new dealer in Augusta. Old World charm subtly flavored with the excitement of Spain, in Pecan. Answer the riddle at the end of Scenario 1 to find out about Borg. I can see you have a lot to learn.

SCENARIO 1: Time: 5:30 P.M., on a Sunday in late November. In the small but neat galley kitchen in the Manhattan apartment of Mrs. Lillian Hasty, a bride of three months, Mrs. Hasty, just returned with her husband from an afternoon at the Museum of

Modern Art, is preparing the evening meal. After a few moments toiling in the kitchen, she serves her husband a packaged onion soup, au gratin, to start. The entree is Mrs. Borg's Swedish Meatballs in Burgundy Sauce on a bed of Minute Rice, accompanied by frozen creamed spinach and salad. A rosé wine and, for dessert, Jell-o topped with a dab of quickie whipped "cream," a favorite garnie of the Hastys', complete the meal. Lillian and Howard dine by candlelight in the foyer of their chic apartment, and Howard eats with gusto, more than once expressing his satisfaction with Lillian's cooking. He burps quietly, however, immediately after eating (a frequent phenomenon of Howard's), and later in the evening spends some time on the toilet, as does Lillian. What did Lillian really serve her husband?

Darling Ian, we should forget about that day in the pool. And you're selling pianos for Jonas, not for me. But he *is* planning a trip to Savannah. I looked in his appointment book. In April. I am being especially sweet and kind to him these days. See, you make *me* good, too. Lillian served Howard among the meatballs hydrolyzed plant protein, disodium inosinate, disodium guanylate, caramel food color, and modified food starch. Burp! Are you a food nut, too?

3

I N February, when the days begin to lengthen into splen-
did fiery sunsets and I can see and feel and smell spring
coming, I naturally feel myself waxing and expanding too,
like the bulbs shooting into green in my garden.

Jonas is always home in the late winter and early spring.
His travels don't start until April, when he sets out for
weeks at a time to his eleven territories, his men in the field.
But in February and March Jonas is home with us every
night; we are complete, a family, and our weekends are
loving and warm and all that a woman could wish for.

The house is of rosy brick, square, light, and pleasant.
We have lived here since Teddy was an infant. We have
two pianos, a baby grand (a Fleming), and a vertical
Steinway (inherited), and four fireplaces, and on Sunday
afternoons in the winter Jonas makes a fire in the living-
room fireplace and plays the piano while I read the paper
and sip a glass of sherry or lie on the floor with the boys
to build trains and towers out of blocks.

The music crashes around us. Jonas plays the piano the
way he does everything else, briskly, with a resolute clatter
and dash that banish doubt. I can't tell whether he plays

well or badly. It sounds good to me and fills my soul with richness and sometimes my eyes with tears. In fact, his playing can, when I'm feeling susceptible, move me more than anything on earth, and on winter Sunday afternoons like these I always feel like the luckiest woman alive.

And, after a while, when the fire has made the room too warm for comfort and we are all restless and itching to move, we bundle ourselves in sweaters and jackets and pull knitted caps down over our ears and charge out into the crisp air. We get a football out of the barn, which we use as a garage, and which has an apartment over it for a chauffeur, if one were unfortunate enough to need such an encumbrance, and run the boys across the lawn and over the stone wall and up the little hill we own next door, high-stepping through the stiff winter grass.

I lie on my back in the grass and listen to the bluejays screaming in the woods and the crows cawing and think how perfect everything is, while the boys tumble down the other side of the hill to retrieve the football Jonas has tossed down for them. They come back to me. Teddy tackles me on the ground, and little Peter laughs with glee from his father's shoulders, so glad he is that we are all together.

We plod happily back to the house, where a chicken roasts in the oven, and as I stand at the sink paring potatoes and washing a crisp green-blue head of broccoli, I wonder how I could ever be disconsolate again. But then I hear Jonas tossing blocks into the toy box, picking up the living room for me, and I know that in the morning they will all be gone again.

Leaving me alone.

My disaffection began in September when Peter started nursery school, when it dawned on me that I had no baby any more, no company in the morning as I puttered around the house, no chum to have a cozy morning snack with, nobody to chat with on the way to the supermarket, when it dawned on me that in fact I had no good reason at all for even *being* in the house most of the day.

In any day of sixteen waking hours in this winter of my discontent, for ten, from half-past nine in the morning until half-past twelve, from one-thirty to five-thirty, and from eight till eleven, I have very little of importance to do and, in the morning, nobody to do it with. The furnace runs for me alone. And I don't even pay for the oil.

Once a week, an untalkative woman with a vexed face comes in and changes the sheets, washes the tiled floors, vacuums, and goes at the woodwork or the refrigerator or the silver, as the need may be. Most of the laundry is sent out. There is very little of anything left for me to do. Jonas approves. He doesn't think his wife should spend all her time on her hands and knees. The other days, I go around the house in the morning after they have all left and toss toys into toy boxes, make the beds, load the dishwasher, distribute the clean laundry. This takes me an hour. At half-past nine I am finished. What do I do?

I do not sew or bake or decorate wastebaskets to match Kleenex boxes. Nor do I work clever crewel toadstools and ladybugs to delight my friends and relations at Christmas. I am not interested in découpage, which some of my friends have taken up. And I have resisted both invitations to join the very active African violet club in town. I am not a clubwoman. I am not a craftswoman. I am not even charity-minded. I say No, not this year, thank you, to all invitations to be the cancer lady on Five-Mile Road, the multiple sclerosis captain, the cystic fibrosis co-chairman. There is a new disease out this year. I have seen it advertised on television. I can't pronounce it, but I have been asked to be county co-chairman of the campaign to eradicate it.

I have not attended any of the consciousness-raising sessions at Connie's house, either.

Just as with philosophy and crafts and charity I am apathetic, so with Great Issues I am apolitical. I care nothing for the rights of women, which she has lately begun to tell me men have been circumscribing since time began. That talk bores me.

I am totally Lilycentric. Like a child, I am easily pleased and easily displeased. And right now it displeases me to have to live only for others—to have to be an appendage to their lives rather than an illumination to my own. My right, it seems to me, is to live first of all for myself, and then for my others.

Jonas sees it the other way around, and this is the source of my resentment. "I want to have a little life of my own, Jonas," I say. "To be *somebody* again. To be plain Lily Ashe. Not Mrs. Jonas Ashe. Not Teddy and Peter Ashe's mother. I simply wish to be a separate and distinct and whole person, living a little life of my own. A compromise, Jonas. Please?"

I want to go back to my job at the library, where, before he moved us out here to northern Westchester, out of all reasonable reach of the city, I was the assistant curator of medieval and Renaissance manuscripts. I long for that quiet job in that quiet place. I long for the beautiful illuminations to pore over, the collections to study, the exhibitions to arrange, the delicacy and excitement of a discovery to make. I identified two pages from two different manuscripts while I was there and a rook to complete the library's only medieval chess set. These findings were all published in *The Journal of Medieval Affairs* (no pun intended, Heloise, et al.). They were not much, but one does not have to discover DNA to make a name for oneself. I was just beginning to make a name for myself when I had to leave.

"It wouldn't be a compromise your way either, Lily," he tells me. "To get there by nine, you'd have to leave here by seven, and that's way before the boys even have to leave. And you wouldn't be back until seven. You wouldn't be a mother any more. You'd be a tired commuter sleeping in our house at night."

"Like you," I reply angrily. "That's what you are." Yet I know he is right. That's what irks me most of all.

"Look," he says, getting fed up with me. "If you want to work, get a little part-time job around here."

"No." I want *my* job.

"You want to have your cake and eat it too. You're a wife and a mother now. If you can find something to do that doesn't interfere with that, fine. Otherwise, forget it."

"You're a tyrant and a bore," I say fiercely through my teeth. "Why should I take a job just to fill my time. Would *you* do that? I want recognition. I want my own job. I want people to say, 'Lily's coming back, just in time. This place was falling to pieces without her.' Don't you understand? I want power and prestige."

"I wish Connie would get laid in the afternoon instead of filling your head with that junk," he says.

Now, how can you reason with a man like that?

So, that's why I cracked the little nut that fell into my palm green in January, and ate the ripening meat. Ian gives me a life of my own.

Part of it is that, that Ian fills a vacuum. And part of it is the strange new energy my secret gives me to spend. I like that. And part of it is Ian himself. I am immensely drawn to him as never to a man before. Capricorn woman

25

and Taurus man. A combination to remember. His large frame that can enfold mine, his quick face, quick to flash signals to me across a room, his animal litheness, what I take to be his highmindedness. I like all that in a man. And part of it, I must admit, is the little pleasure of getting back at Jonas for keeping me down on the farm.

Ian gives me a private and a secret life that has nothing to do with anything else. My days build themselves around the mailman's coming, and he comes two or three times a week with mail from Savannah.

Impatient, I sometimes wait for him on my bike at the end of the driveway, and one day I think he looks at me in a certain way when he hands me the letter. You must stop mailing all your letters from Savannah, I write. Sprinkle them around a bit. Beaufort, Augusta, Charleston, Tampa, Orlando. Discretion, at any price. *Darling*. This is all for today. The mommies are coming for lunch. Lobster newburg and frozen coconut cream pie. Yum!

My Darling Dummy, you could give all the moms in Westchester a tummy ache they'd never forget with frozen coconut cream pie, he writes back. Answer the riddle at the end of Scenario 2.

SCENARIO 2: Time: Noon. The well-appointed home of Mrs. Hardy overlooking San Francisco Bay. Mrs. H. is bustling about the kitchen putting the finishing touches on the luncheon she will shortly be serving to her bridge club.

After a few hands of bridge, the twelve ladies partake of lobster newburg, a molded gelatin salad, and coconut cream pie, expertly thawed. They are all thrilled by the menu, at least judging by the glad cries that accompany each course. But an hour after eating

Mrs. X. feels unpleasant rumblings in her lower intestine and has to excuse herself. Shortly after this, Mrs. Z., a newcomer to the club, feels disgraced by an indelicate odor.

What made Mrs. Z. fart?

You *are* a food nut! Mrs. Z. farted because she ate hydrogenated vegetable oil, water, flour, sugar, vegetable shortening, graham flower, corn syrup, coconut, nonfat dry milk solids, starch, brown sugar, sodium caseinate, invert sugar, salt, lecithin, honey, molasses, leavening, gelatin, cellulose gum, mono- and diglycerides, glycerol lacto, esters, and artificial flavors and colors. Mothers! Forgive me!

I answer every letter I get, taking care to vary my own hand and stationery, though he has assured me that Savannah has thousands of post-office boxes and that postmen are a breed whose genetic makeup leaves them notoriously inattentive to the intrigues that daily pass through their hands. Still, one takes no chances with one's other life, for that is of course the more important one.

Tall Lily, blond and decorous, I join an exercise class at the Y. Who knows? The time may come when all of my thirty-four-year-old body will be exposed to a twenty-eight-year-old eye, though I am sure that is a possibility with only the barest chance of becoming reality. I brush my hair furiously to make it shine, and I wonder whether to have my ears pierced. I feel I am not beautiful enough, or young enough, or *modern* enough for Ian. But having one's ears pierced is an irrevocable act.

I am happier these days. I begin to whistle while I work, speeding through the familiar chores with, for me, an unnatural vim. And I hug and squeeze my boys more than usual and romp with them over the frozen lawn in the weak noon sun. They love their bouncy new Mom. And I love Ian and the attention he gives me. It makes me feel like somebody.

As usual, I play with them after their naps, read to them, and on rainy days, boil salt and cornstarch on the stove for them, producing a modeling dough that we mold into alligators and monsters. As usual, when it rains or snows, I get out the paste and make sticky collages with them from the scrap box I keep, or pipe-cleaner puppets. And I make endless Tinker Toy constructions with them, and I take them in the car to play with Connie's children, or Jo-Anne's, while we moms compare notes over instant coffee in mugs about *their* development, about our husbands' careers, about our own so-modest hopes and dreams. And in the evenings, of course, as usual there is Jonas. I feed him and wine him and listen to him and talk to him. All these things I have always done. But now always, always, no matter what I do these days, in a secret part of me another activity is going on. My dialogue with Ian. That is what I *do*.

He is becoming a major occupation. I write to him, I diet and exercise for him, I examine labels at the supermarket for him. I perfect my penmanship for him, my beautiful Italic hand. I even buy a new nib, extra-fine straight, for my Osmiroid pen for him. I read and reread his letters. And I look in the mirror to see how he sees me. I am falling in love with him. That's what I do. I happily squander my days on him.

He has come along at a time in my life when, in my own way and at my own speed, I have been trying to break out of the box I have lived in looking out of since my childhood. The winds of other people's liberation have been whistling past my head for some time, and I sometimes hear myself, inside my head, shout, Me too, I want to be in on all this too. But I am not even sure of what it is I want to be a part of. And perhaps if I were I would not want to be a part of it after all.

My reaching out to try things I have never tried before antedated Ian. But he is part of it. He has reinforced it.

I am an anachronism in the world I live in. Most people I know do things nowadays that I have never done, or have just learned to do. I have just recently learned to drive a car, for instance. It is hard to imagine how one could live up here and not know, yet I did it, for four years, riding my bike to the village with Teddy on the seat behind, and having the groceries and liquor and hardware and dry cleaning delivered. But having Peter made that too complicated, so I learned to drive.

It wasn't easy, at thirty-two, any more than learning to ski was easy at thirty-two, or learning to ice skate. Yet I have learned both of those things in the last few years. And I don't have weak ankles, as I had always believed, nor am I too clumsy and cerebral, as I had also always been told, for sports. Jonas, a born athlete, tells me I have wonderful coordination and would have made a good girl athlete if I'd tried. I do gay mental flips at such praise.

I have also learned to read a road map, and I can identify all the hoses and valves and knobs and containers under the hood of the car, and if my station wagon should stall or boil over or smoke or steam or not want to start, I can open the hood and prod at filters and twist knobs and even go at the spark plugs with a can of spray I have and get it started. It's a whole new world for me, the world of cars. And the newest thing about it is: the car radio! Ian taught me about that.

I know that some people's cars are equipped with cassettes and stereos and tape decks and speakers in the back seat, but for me it was a breakthrough just to drive with the *radio* on. My father never did it, and Jonas can't stand popular music, which is all that seems to come out of car radios, so it was not until Ian described to me how he put ABC on loud and streaked down Route 1 with me on his mind that I tried it for myself. On the Merritt Parkway.

I like it. It makes me feel so good and so alive that I can hardly stand myself. It sets me on fire to do what the music is all about. Ian, did you know it would do that?

I sometimes recite the following history to myself when I try to understand how it is that in 1970 I hardly know what is going on in the new world around me and have been no part of it, how it is that, to me, *Ian* is the new world.

I am an only child. I grew up in rural Connecticut, and we had no car at all until well after the war was over. We had no need of one. Everyone we knew lived in the town, including all our relatives. We also knew everyone who lived in it, which isn't to say the same thing. We did have a radio, and like our black table-model telephone, it was a major "piece" in the living room. It stood on the floor, big and brown and round and hooded like a monk whose eyes, green and amber, lit up when he was turned on. It spluttered and cracked and gave out war news, which my mother listened to but did not hear (it is from her that I get my Lilycentric notions), and dance-band music and on Saturday nights Frank Sinatra and the hit parade. I think that was the most intimate I ever became with mass culture.

I had a comfortable and secure childhood. Advanced nearsightedness kept my father at home through the whole war, and I had cousins to play with and aunts to confide in. In those days adults tried to shelter children from the

realities of life. Today we try to give them a social con-
science while they're still in diapers. Maybe it will help to
make a better world.

Up to the time I went to New York for my interview
at Barnard, I had never spent a night out of Goshen.

My Barnard years were nearly as quiet as my home years.
I was highminded, there for an education, and pure, admiring among men only certain professors and such public
figures as Sir John Gielgud and Edmund Wilson.

After a year getting a master's degree in fine arts at
Columbia, I went to the library, and there my life went
on, as cloistered still as a nun's. Then I met Jonas—at a
concert of medieval music in the library courtyard: where
else?—and we were married a year later. He is almost as
behind the times as I am. We have always liked it that way.

A Jewish piano salesman was not what my mother and
father had gone without for, they indicated. His family, on
the other hand, who lived in a green and expensive ghetto
on Long Island, was as disappointed in me as I was in them.
Our antipathy never caused Jonas any grief, however; they
died shortly after our wedding in an automobile crash
on the Long Island Expressway.

Jonas and his brother sold the house and with the money
bought their own in waspy neighborhoods for their waspy
wives. It is just amazing how this turn of events enhanced
Jonas's image in Goshen.

I am content with Jonas, I suppose, though our minds
perhaps have never been totally engaged, or, sometimes I
think, our bodies either, and maybe for that very reason.

But these are female complaints, and no cause for alarm.
I wonder about it though, and if there is some lack in me.
Still, they say that the Capricorn woman finds it difficult
to express her feelings or to respond to love, and so in the

last analysis I attribute many such things in me to the stars.

My other problem, my being so out of step with the age I live in, takes precedence right now, in my catalog of topics for concern, because I have the feeling that my coming to grips with modern times is going to mean my coming to grips with myself, going to mean changing my comfortable self in some uncomfortable way. And that is the thing about it that I am not sure I want to do.

4

LYING on a beach in a faraway place and talking to a man not one's husband is one thing, and agreeing to write letters to him is yet another, for one can always change one's mind about that, but getting phone calls from him in one's own house adds a third dimension, and I was surprised that the one thing led to the others so quickly.

I think I expected that my being married, and married at that to the man who had hired him, would make me unapproachable, once I was out of his physical range. But what ever made me think that? He approached me on the beach in plain view of the hotel windows where Jonas was discussing The Role of the Regional Manager, or Sales Strategy for the Seventies, or Profits vs. Prestige: Whither F & F? Why did I ever imagine he would hesitate to approach me on the telephone?

What is there about me? I want to ask him. What is there that makes you do this? But the corollary is, What is there about you, Lily, that makes *you* do it? And that question I do not yet want to put to myself.

I came home from Florida with the idea that we would

write a few times during the year and that the following year we would meet again in Palm Beach and perhaps engage briefly on a dark terrace on the last night, and I was content to fantasize along these romantic lines. But the astonishing thing was that everything moved so much more quickly than that. And now I am caught up in a whirlwind of letters and phone calls, and I have learned to dissemble and to deceive Jonas with a deftness that makes me marvel. It is easy to do.

How much money do you spend on phone calls, Ian? Do you charge them to the company? I never ask. I have so quickly come to take them for granted, a part of my week, then a pivot for a day, that I never think of them as having a value in monetary terms. His voice, so eager and charged, raises me from the dead. That is all that matters.

Don't lovers always know when the phone will ring? I take no chance when I pick up the phone and say, simply, Hi. I know, after two weeks, when it will be he. He tells me this is because we have good vibrations, so good in fact that we should put them to work. And so we set on a time each day for mental concentration, and the time is early in the morning.

That is how it happened that in my king-sized bed in my king-sized bedroom, lying next to my little king-sized husband, I desired Ian. It was impossible, in these sur- roundings, lying so softly and warmly in my so-recently- vanished sleep, not to imagine that he lay there next to me, sharing my pillow, while on the other pillow, his back to us, Jonas struggled against waking, giving us perfect freedom. First our fingers mingled and then we kissed, eyes open and lips parted, but chastely dry, and then one morning he indicated that enough was enough, and I opened for him. Oh, Lily, to think of what you did. But it was bliss, and if my cheeks flamed, it was only I who knew why. Not even Ian ever knew.

Adultery. Though my body is, was, Presbyterian, my soul is and always will be pre-Reformation. To imagine the sin is to have committed the sin. That's what the Bible says. I have known him in my heart.

This makes me rather hangdog around Jonas, who is good to me.

"You look beautiful tonight, Lily," he says one March evening, coming in from work through the back door into the kitchen where I stand shaking a saucepan of brussels sprouts.

I kiss him on his nose without even leaving my sprouts. Jonas is my height, five feet ten, and chubby. He throws his chest out and struts when he walks, like a conductor walking out to the podium, or like the Little King in the funny papers walking out to his balcony to wave to his subjects. He has a bemused expression on his face most of the time, but Jonas is never bemused. He is only thinking, the wheels inside his head turning, turning. How can he make more money for Fleming & Fleming? How can he squeeze more sales out of the franchise holders? How can he get his wife and sons to grow up the way he wants them to? How can he fit in a game of squash and still make the 5:38? How can he have the best lawn in town and still do all the other things he does? He hangs up his coat and hat and kisses me back, on the neck. "You must be in love," he says.

"Then you must be my lover," I answer, and that night I twine my long legs around his with special warmth so he will be sure that he is.

My husband sleeps. My house sleeps. I lie awake and think of Ian. I try to remember what he looks like. I remember his hair, long, fluffing nicely around his collar, and I remember his eyes gray and warm. His nose I cannot remember at all, except vaguely that it is smashed in some way, or his mouth either. Or his ears, but they are not important. I remember how big he is, bigger than Jonas. And I remember how nimble he was and how agile at volleyball in the sand under the coconut trees. And how we danced and kept encountering each other unexpectedly under palm trees and at turnings of the hotel corridors. Ian! The looks we traded.

It is hard for me to believe he is married. His spirits are so high.

But then, it is hard for me to believe I am married any more. I am leading two lives, and in my Ian life I am the girl I never was in Lily-days gone by.

I lie awake in the dark and think of him and touch my body. I think of Savannah and April and of coming together with him.

Jonas stirs. Do my thoughts wake him? Or is it the thumping of my heart? How can he lie in bed with me, my husband, and not hear what is going on in my head?

Jonas, Jonas, can't you hear me, what I'm saying? Wake up. Wake up. I think I am trying to tell you something.

Teddy coughs and cries out for me in the dark. His cough is thick and phlegmy in his chest. He is prone to bronchitis.

I put them both out this afternoon, and I shouldn't have. It was a raw, gray day, and they had colds. But they were caroming into my Ian reverie, and so I shoved them angrily into snowcoats and put them out.

I lie still, hoping he will go back to sleep, but soon he calls again, and cries. I slip out of bed and down the hall to him in my bare feet. I hold him on my lap on the edge of the bed. His head is hot. I give him two little orange-flavored aspirin and a teaspoon of cough syrup. I know that in the morning he will need to see the doctor.

This makes me very angry with myself. I see now what I am doing. My preoccupation with him fills me with disgust. It has got to end.

In the morning I write to him. Ian, I say, for one thing, the telepathy has to go. Erotic thoughts of you are beginning to take over my life. I was willing only to be Laura, but our relationship has lately begun to smack of an earlier convention, and we must either reverse the carnal trend or stop communicating altogether. Besides, am I a woman so poor in spirit that a perfect stranger can alter my life and even my looks and my personality merely by walking up to me on the beach?

A perfect stranger. Perfect, but no stranger. I know him.

Dearest Laura, he returns, If I had to give you up now my life would fall in shreds around my feet. Understand what you mean to me. You lighten my dismal existence, you give me hope. You make me bearable to my family. You regenerate me. You make me *good*, darling. I don't want to make you unhappy. Down with sex. Who needs it anyway. Please don't stop writing. I have to have your letters.

Seen in this light, what can be wrong? We *are* platonic lovers only. There is no need to be anxious. Not even Jonas could object. Besides, I say to myself, I can have a friend, can't I?, even while recognizing the words as Daisy Buchanan's and even though recalling that Laura died of the plague.

And so, I have a friend. My secret life goes on. It absorbs me and fills my life and my mind like air filling a balloon. But, still, I have thought the unthinkable, I have dwelt on it in my heart, and things will never be the same again. Even though I am still the irreproachable wife, I have crossed in some subtle way into a gray limbo between the order of a perfect union and the rebellion implicit in an imperfect one.

Sometimes such thoughts drive me out of doors, and I climb the little knoll and look back at my square rosy box of a house of which a widely read book assures me I am the "warm, ever-love-giving, never-failing center of approval —the heart."

And, I think, that's the trouble. I *am* the heart of it. Wife. Mother. Warm, ever-love-giving center. What would they do without me? But even now they are without me, because I am never fully here any more.

I am supposed to be the heart of it. But at the same time I am the canker in it. Irritable, easily angered, I am an affliction to my sons and a bristle in my husband's side.

I long for spring, hoping that with the passing of the monotonous winter, my temper will improve. But spring is forever in coming, and I end by going to it before it comes to me.

5

BEFORE we get to Savannah, where we are scheduled to spend one night and one day, I have to endure stopovers in Richmond, Raleigh, and Spartanburg, South Carolina.

Imagine my sensations upon arriving in Savannah. I am in such a state of high tension at the thought of seeing him again that I scream aloud at a backfiring car. Then I leave my coat in the taxi on the way to the hotel. I never see it again. I think now I meant to leave it, to represent what else I wanted to leave.

Imagine too my sensations at being sprung again out of the winter, for though we are well into April and past Easter, it is still winter in New York. I leave all that winter can be in April up there, slush and tattered snowcoats, and odd mittens, and I emerge from the plane into a warm and scented and heady spring. The shock is felt.

In the taxi Jonas talks about a tone problem in the high octaves on the new French Provincial vertical, mentioning pinblocks and bridges, but I lie back and wonder at trees in leaf and southern gardens.

I feel as if I am about to be ejected from a sealed capsule into space. Yet I feel dread also. The burdens of winter and separation are lifted, but I am suddenly afraid to see him.

In the hotel room in Savannah, I insist on taking a shower. "There isn't time," Jonas objects. "It's quarter to seven now." I close the bathroom door on his voice and lock it. I hear him banging on it as I step under the hot needle spray. I shower quickly, just to wash the smell of airports from my skin. I rub myself dry in front of the mirror. My skin is pink from the friction. Jonas bangs on the door again. "Let me in. I have to go," he shouts. I throw a palmful of cologne on my throat and breasts. I feel exhilarated, as if I am getting ready to go out on a date. I wrap a towel around myself and let him in, and close the door on him again, so I can be alone in the capacious room they have given us to look at myself a second time.

I recall having been told that my grandfather was vacationing in this famous hotel the night I was born. Only now it has been taken over by a chain and renovated and does not in any way resemble the Victorian grandeur of the place my grandfather described.

I drop my towel and walk across the room toward the cheval glass. I am pretty. I am amazed at how pretty. We have no full-length mirror at home, so I rarely see all of myself at once. Tonight, I want someone to share the vision, to tell me that my breasts stand up, that my long legs unmarred by veins move with a gawky girlishness from the hip, that my thighs will never shiver and shake with bubbles of fat. But I hear Jonas coming. It will not do to stir him up. I move quickly into my gym-prim underwear and put on lipstick and a green cowled chiffon dress that flutters around me as we step out of the elevator.

We are to meet in the bar. He is there first. I begin to tremble and shake when I see him. He looks different from the way I remember him. I am disappointed and cannot look at his face. His clothes. His hair. He is more what they call mod than I remember. I am so what they call suburban.

But soon we are laughing and talking and forgetting that Jonas and Becky are there. Becky is trying hard to act the way she imagines Ian wants her to act, but she calls Jonas Mr. Ashe. Jonas is busy being the expansive host, ordering drinks, then something to nibble on, as he puts it, and cigarettes, and more drinks. "Call us Lily and Jonas," I say quickly the next time. She blushes. I feel Ian growing still. He is afraid I am going to patronize her. I am afraid I am too. I remember what he said in Palm Beach. "I shouldn't talk about her. Out of respect." She *is* his wife.

"Will you have lunch with me tomorrow?" I ask her. "And show me around Savannah?" She would love to, she says. Her eyes gleam briefly, like those of a furry animal caught in the beam of a flashlight.

We have another round of drinks and then two bottles of wine with our dinner, and Ian convulses us with stories about life in Savannah. I haven't laughed so hard in years.

But when he mentions that he comes from Pittsburgh, I am sobered for a moment by the realization of how very little I know about this man who has gotten on the inside of my head. From Pittsburgh to Savannah. That explains his incredulity at southerners and southern mores. "There's a big thing going on right now in the state legislature about whether to build a new mental hospital in Georgia," he says. And then, "Hell," he says, "they don't need a new asylum down here. All they need to do is put a fence around Savannah."

We laugh and laugh and I comb his face with my eyes

so I will remember it afterwards. His hair is shorter than in January but still down around his collar, and his eyes are gray and keen and flood me with light. His nose has been broken, and his mouth draws my eye all evening.

Becky likes the South. She believes it is a good place to bring up daughters. "They learn the true feminine role down here and don't get confused by having to compete with boys," she says. "In the South, girls are protected from the sordid aspects of life up North and are encouraged to develop their natural domestic and motherly instincts."

"Very protected," says Ian, and tells a story about his brother's child, a northerner, who visited them in Savannah over Easter. "He was swinging on a monkey swing in the back yard," says Ian. "It has a circular seat suspended from a rope. After a while he jumped off and announced to us all that he didn't like the swing because the seat hurt his balls, whereupon my innocent eldest daughter said proudly, 'It doesn't hurt *my* balls,' and hopped on the swing."

"Really, Ian," says Becky.

We all laugh again at this very funny story, but in the back of my mind I am thinking about . . . balls. And what goes with them.

Finally, Jonas says it's time to call it a day. "Got to get an early start on the yokels tomorrow, boy."

"Yeah," says Ian. "We've got a lot of cages out there to rattle." Salesmen's talk. He touches my arm as we move out of the dining room, behind Jonas and Becky. We look at each other.

There is a kind of peace in his face. "I'll see you," he says. I swell with joy at the thought. He is to migrate to my migraine tomorrow night.

I have breakfast brought to me in bed in the morning after Jonas has left to meet Ian, whom he "loves." Jonas is effusive, like a television talk-show star. "That Ian. What a beautiful guy. What a lovely person," he says as he dresses. "I love him. He's the greatest. Do you know what I mean? Isn't he something else?"

"Yes," I say. "Very nice." Jonas wears boxer shorts, but I imagine that Ian wears the others.

My breakfast comes to me elaborately on a cart with a rose and a copy of the morning paper and a pot of coffee and six different dishes all covered with silver-plated domes. I find oatmeal, a soft-boiled egg, sausages, home fries, grits, and hot muffins puddled with butter. I eat the egg and the sausage and try the grits but don't like their blandness. I have the muffins and coffee and read the paper to see what is going on in Ian's town. Then after a while I put the paper away and slip back under the covers to dwell on him and to wonder what will happen tonight.

Finally, I get up and dress and visit a house described as America's finest example of English Regency architecture; it has a walled garden in the back, and a fragrance of plants unknown to me wafts in through the tall windows. I think of mimosa and mulberry. But mulberries, I recall, are fed to pigs and chickens. They would not be here. Pomegranate? I think of a woodcut at the library: Mary holding a pomegranate, symbol of hope and fertility. The house has a bridge across the upstairs hall, but visitors are not permitted to walk across it. I think of other bridges I will cross today.

At noon, I wander into their street, fifteen minutes early. That is fourteen too many to take in the neighborhood, which the general lack of paint suggests is one of rental properties. But it is pleasant in a faded way, though there are no sidewalks and I must pick my way down the street through a dozen tricycling preschoolers out to meet their sisters and brothers coming home for lunch. The little girls walk two-by-two, chatting earnestly, and I wonder which among all the blonds are Ian's.

I realize as soon as I get to the house what a lot of trouble my largesse has put Becky to. She is not used to going out for lunch, and she has had to make arrangements this morning for the first-grader to have lunch at a friend's house near school, and for the three-year-old and the baby to have lunch at a neighbor's, and for the older one to go to that neighbor's after school. She is harassed and ill at ease, but she asks me in to wait in the house while she hustles, pretty and plump and curly, across the back yards with her little ones. I feel ill at ease too, and too modish in my matching yellow and gray plaid dress and coat and smart calf shoes from Bergdorf's. I take off my boater and look at my reflection in the glass hanging in the little front hall. I look intense and intent, as indeed I am to see his house. I smooth my bangs and tuck my straight shining hair behind my ears and tell myself to calm down.

It is a deep-porched, squat, two-story cottage such as one sees in southern towns; palmetto palms shade it closely, and when I step into the living room it is a moment before my eyes adjust to the dim interior. It is neat and clean, though the woodwork is chipped beyond redemption. It is balanced as carefully as a motel room with its trim, prim gold tweed couch and chairs and matched end tables and coffee table all set down on the brown tweed carpeting as if by an unseen hand firmly taught the correct way to arrange furniture in a room. Twin lamps and matching ash trays do not remind me of Ian.

There is nothing of him in the room, or in the dining room either, which is carrying an old mahogany table and chairs and sideboard that are far too heavy for it. I wish

44

his guitar case were leaning against the end of the sideboard, but it is not, and I wonder at her urge to obscure him so completely in her design. For a moment I picture an oil of him surfing nude at Waikiki over the sideboard, or at least a pile of his clean laundry folded on the table waiting to be carried upstairs. But there is nothing. I hear her coming back. I sit down quickly on the foam rubber couch.

Lunch is Ian-this and Ian-that. And Ian is doing so well this year, and Ian is so good with the girls these days. Ian my eye, I feel like saying. You are not the keeper of Ian's eye, my dear. I am Ian's eye's keeper now.

"But, of course," she is saying, stabbing her Jello salad, "it all means you can't mind playing second fiddle, doesn't it?"

"Second fiddle?" I fear she is going to make some horrible woman-to-woman revelation. My shrimp creole loses its minor appeal.

"To his job." She looks directly at me with very clear eyes. "You must have the same thing."

"Oh, yes. Yes. Jonas is very involved. I wish I could get *my* teeth into something." Besides this tough shrimp. I am relieved.

"Do you mean a job?" she asks. "What about your little boys?"

"My little boys are in school all morning."

"I don't believe in women working when they have little ones at home," she says.

"It's not everyone's cup of tea," I reply diplomatically.

"It's not mine," she says, digging into her tapioca. "I think Mom is doing the very best thing in the world she can do by giving her children the security of knowing she's at home waiting for them whenever they might need her.

Love is what mother means. Not bringing home money."

"Well," I say, "time is life. That's my philosophy. And we should be able to do more than one thing at a time." Have more than one man at a time, for instance. "Wasted time is wasted life."

"You're an intellectual," she says. "You need more."

Yes, Becky.

After lunch we drive in her car to the restored area along the river, but her chatter soon wears me down. After a tour of the Trustees Garden and the oldest house in Georgia, I tell her, again diplomatically, I hope, that I have to go. She is disappointed that we will not be able to "do" the Historical Society. Now I will miss seeing the musket ball that felled General Pulaski.

For no reason at all, I wish her luck when we part. Luck at what, she may well have wondered. She isn't doing anything but loving, and she's had all the luck she needs at that. Hasn't Ian left her twice and gone back twice?

I try my best to persuade Jonas to go on to Atlanta without me, but he insists on staying. There is no point in arguing with him; he is as hard to shake as a burr. So, I send him out to get a prescription for Darvon filled, and while he is gone I call Ian. We have anticipated Jonas and have a second plan. I let the phone ring once and hang up. Then I dial a second time. He answers on the first ring. Plan II, I say, and hang up. If Becky asks, he will say it was a wrong number.

When Jonas returns, I order him to go to a movie so I can be alone with my aching head. This much I know he will do.

Fifteen minutes later, I meet Ian in the bar. We know we are taking a chance, but we have an alibi all ready. It would be riskier to go out to another place, or to have him in the room. And as for that, I am not really ready yet to

46

have him in my room, to put my body on the line. I want to talk to him first, before I decide.

It doesn't matter that we have two hours instead of twenty-two. We say what we have to say.

"I think about you all my waking hours."

"I know. I know. I do the same."

"You obsess me."

"I know. It's the same with me."

"What shall we do?"

"I'll never leave Jonas."

"I couldn't ask you to. I'll never do it to Becky again either."

"Was there somebody else the other times? Does she suspect anything now?" We speak hurriedly, filling in the gaps in our information for each other. There are some questions we do not even take the time to answer, so avid are we to get to the point.

"I'm madly in love with you," he says, and I feel so gratified I could cry. I tell him the same thing. He extends a finger to caress the back of my hand.

I watch his finger stroke, but I don't say anything. I want him to say it.

"What shall we do then?" he asks again.

"Keep on?" He makes *me* do it.

He nods.

The matter is settled then, and relieved of it we drink our drinks and talk about other things for a while. I ask him why he has no piano in his house, and he tells me that he has one but keeps it locked in a room upstairs, because Becky let the dog gnaw on its legs.

"Doesn't the dog obey you?"

"The dog? The kids don't even obey me. She spoils them. They're all she has."

"And you?"

"I have you."

When we leave he walks with me to the elevator. "I'll get to New York this summer," he says. "Some way." Behind a column he passes his mouth over mine. Dry. We like it and try it again. I am faint when I step into the elevator.

In the morning I say good-bye to Jonas at the airport. His plane leaves for Atlanta at the same time as mine leaves for New York. He praises the Darvon. I feel just great today, Jonas.

6

AT home again I change. I am gay and happy, my eye focused on summer. The household relaxes. The day after I get back Jonas returns for the weekend to rest before taking off for another two weeks, this time in the Midwest.

It is a good weekend, full of loving and doing things all together, the four of us, with Ian in the background watching me out of his calmness.

It does not bother me at all that I have entered into a compact with another man. I have segregated that right out of my life with Jonas. It belongs to my other life, my secret life, and I feel I have every right in the world to have it that way. It is simple and clear in my mind, and it makes me very happy.

I sing and dance for my men and fool and laugh. They love it when I act the warm ever-love-giving center. But all the while my secret life binds me in an ever-stronger tie outside the house. I plot. I dream. I sit in my deep armchair in a corner of the kitchen and smile at my spice rack, or cock my head to listen to a voice in the middle distance. Ian is talking to me.

Sunny and warm and splashed with red and yellow tulips and deep scallops of purple ajuga and grape hyacinth, the two days of our weekend are unexpected bliss after the grim so-long winter. We bask in the sun, feeling strength flow back into our winter-enfeebled bodies, and listen to the boys thrashing through the woods below in search of frogs and dinosaur tracks.

I let everything go in the house to be outside in the sun. The grass has turned a brilliant green overnight and dances with sun and darkens with shifting beautiful shadows.

We spread an army blanket on the back lawn and have lunch out there on Saturday and talk about the wood porch that squares out an ell off the kitchen at the back of the house and that is going to be removed this week because termites have undermined the footings.

Termites have eaten the insides out of the joists and the two-by-fours holding up the porch, leaving on the surface a thin varnished skin that to the untutored eye looks perfectly normal.

My eye has been tutored by the man from the termite company, who taught me to poke through the thin skin of varnish to uncover the white soft-bodied insects eating away inside: the workers and the soldiers, the reproducers and the young, and the rot all around them. "Things are not always what they seem," he said. "You got a nice-looking house, but this part here is full of rot."

Jonas has plans for the ell. "Let's have a big curving redwood deck built," he says, "with a gas-fueled grill. We can eat out there all summer."

"No," I say flatly. "Eating out is only more work for me. And besides it's far too hot on this side of the house, and it's too buggy. And if you roof it and screen it in then it's a porch again. So what's the point?"

"What about having some steps built coming down out of the kitchen and laying a nice flagstone patio?"

"We already have a nice flagstone patio. We never use it."

He keeps thinking.

I lie on my stomach on the blanket and study the ell and think about the man from the termite company.

"Don't feel so bad," he said. "The best families have them. It's no stigma any more. You just protect against it. Routine maintenance nowadays."

We have taken his advice and have had the soil all around the house and the barn poisoned with chlordane. He said it was no stigma any more, so I wondered why they came in unmarked trucks and why the return address on the envelope he sent the bill in read only NYTC. Does the post office know that stands for New York Termite Control?

"I'd like to have that door from the kitchen to the porch bricked in," I say after a while. "That would give us some extra wall space in the kitchen to cork a wall for the boys' schoolwork. And then we can build a walled garden coming out from the house. I saw one in Savannah." Mimosa and pomegranate. That is what I will have.

"What's a walled garden?"

"Don't you remember them from England?"

"No."

He remembers nothing from England, our honeymoon there a tour of ruined abbeys, damp cloisters, royal river palace. I was having a wonderful time, hardly noticing Jonas at all in my delight at seeing Canterbury and Tintern Abbey and Hampton Court and all the rest for the first time, until one day under the ancient grapevine in the palace courtyard he stopped in his tracks and bellowed for all to hear, "I'm bored out of my mind. Let's *do* something!" We hurriedly bought bathing suits and left for the Riviera, where he calmed down in the sun. He has repressed all of England.

"We could extend the kitchen wall of the house a few feet," I muse, "and then build a wall on the other side out about nine feet from the southeast corner of the house, and lay a brick lawn in a herringbone pattern with a diamond shape left in the center for a travertine birdbath, or a little herb bed."

He does not like the idea, but I embroider it in my mind all the afternoon, while he is traversing the lawn with his new green seeding machine and edging the azalea beds with his special sharp edger. My Little King.

The brick wall of the house will be its back and the fourth side will be built up only to a height of three or four feet to let in as much sun as possible. Snug and sheltered, it will be my private place to sit and dwell on Ian and read his letters and the recipes he sends me, even on the most blustery days of the fall and spring, as long as there is sun. I have a quick picture of us there in a double sleeping bag snacking on pignolia nuts. He is playing his recorder, and I am browsing through a facsimile edition of the *Hours of Catherine of Cleves.*

For some reason, I have the idea that Ian and I are timeless and will go on for seasons, never affecting anyone or anything. I forget my biology these days, or is it my medieval theology I am forgetting, that everything affects everything else, in the great chain of being? Whatever it is, I do forget it. It is Ian and I and how we are going to arrange things that matters.

On Monday morning, the first thing I do after the boys leave for school and Jonas for Minneapolis is to call a mason. He drops by on his lunch hour and when I tell him my plan, he shrugs and says, Why not?

He returns in a day with a truckload of rosy brick to match the old brick of the house. He digs the footings and teaches me how to mix mortar and lay brick. I am an apt learner, being highly motivated.

He leaves me an instrument of his that acts like a finger in stroking the mortar between the bricks into submission. It has an effect on me, that thing. It drives me crazy for Ian.

He goes away, returning only at intervals to check on my progress. Up go the walls, brick upon brick, row upon row. I leave cunning little apertures here and there in the walls for the boys to peek through and hide their treasures in. They are still the most important thing in my life, though Ian is vying for their position.

I work every day all day for two weeks, on my knees at first in the soft earth spongy from the melted snows and spring rains, then in a crouching sort of stoop for a week while I lay the middle rows, and then standing at easy working height in the warm afternoon sun of April to do the rows that finally cut off my view of the greening oaks and hickories at the bottom of the fields we call our lawn.

I work slowly, taking care with the mortar to spread it evenly and to get the bricks in their proper stagger. I am in no hurry; I want it to be perfect.

When it is finished I have built a space for myself in the sun, yet out of it; in the air, yet out of the wind; a place to sit and think of Ian whose image is laid in every brick of the enclosure.

I buy a pear tree and three rose bushes to espalier on the south wall and basil and thyme for an herb diamond in the center, and parsley and sage for the borders. Pomegranates are not hardy this far north. Then I move a green wooden high-backed love seat into my little garden, and I sit there and admire it in the April sun. I sit and sit and sit. I read romantic poetry. I think of him and of how it could be. I plan to read his horoscope and mine there every day, because it tells me we are meant for each other. He is the ideal mate for the cold and undemonstrative Capricorn woman. "His strong love and patience should break down her reserve and make her flower into the warm and loving woman she can be under the right circumstances."

In short, I am going madly, madly into love with him.

7

CONNIE lies on her brown velvet couch under a cloud of tobacco smoke. The afternoon sun drops in bars on her Oriental rug.

"I'll have to ask Jonas," I say. "I'll let you know when he gets back on Saturday."

"Jonas. Jonas. What is he, some kind of tyrant around your house?"

I shrug. "I have to ask him. I'm sorry. Anyway, it's against the law, so I'm not too interested."

She dips her finger in her wine and tastes it, smiling into her glass. "You're more sickeningly moralistic than usual today, Lily, my love. What have you been up to?"

"Nothing." My innocence is perfectly feigned. Ian has sent me some seeds from his own *cannabis sativa* to start in my vegetable garden among the string beans and cucumbers and spinach he has encouraged me to grow this year. I wouldn't dream of doing it, of course.

She squints at me over the rim of her wine glass. She is not sure of me today. "You're so out of it," she decides to say. "Forty million Americans are smoking it, and you're not interested."

"Nobody *I* know is, except you." And Ian.

I get up off the floor to look out the windows at the boys. Teddy and Connie's Adam are wrestling in the autumn leaves the melted snow has exposed, and Peter and little Florence are playing in the winter-dirtied sandbox, their curly blond heads uncovered in the mild afternoon sun. Everyone is blond in my world, except Jonas, who is dark and ruddy and bristling at five o'clock.

It is the end of April. He has been gone the whole month, except for that one weekend.

I am very unhappy when he goes away. I feel rootless and unsettled, and uneasy. At night I am sleepless, or sleep fitfully, waking to hear men breaking into the house and creeping up the stairs with hatchets raised to deface my sons and splash me all over the trellised wallpaper. And in the day, it seems to me I subtly take on the postures and ways of a man, clumping about in desert boots and jeans, throwing on Jonas's lumber jacket when I run out in the evening to put bikes and wagons away in the barn for the night. I am the man of the house. I do not like it. "Where did you get it, when we were in college?"

"Remember Billy Butler?"

"Oh, yes. I couldn't stand that freak."

"*You* were the freak, dean's list."

"Thanks, English prize."

She grins. "I love you anyway."

She is my one true friend.

"Did you smoke it when you lived in Washington?"

"Of course. What do you think?" She plays with her long blond hair, twisting it into a rope, piling it on her head. I think of her doing it in the dining room of her Georgetown house while J. Edgar Hoover peers in the window.

She knows what I am thinking. "You're hopeless," she

says. "They were probably growing it in the White House garden, for Christ's sake." I have another image, of Jackie, dressed in blue lady-gardener overalls, a wicker rose basket on her arm, checking her hemp plants for Japanese beetles.

"I know I'm behind the times," I say. "It all comes from my sheltered childhood. Did I ever tell you that I was the only kid in town who wasn't allowed to go to the Saturday matinee?"

"Yeah."

"Or drink soda? Or read comics? Or play kick-the-can in the street after supper?"

"You've told me all that. Don't bore me . . . You have to rise above your repressive past. Get liberated."

"Have you had any lovers since you've been married?" I could bite my tongue. Now what made me ask her *that*, of all things? Especially now when she's just been reading me an article accusing American women of being overly interested in their vaginas, what goes into them and what comes out of them. "Do you agree with this?" she demanded, dealing the magazine a karate chop.

Yes. I do agree.

"That's why I *dig* you, Lily. You never *bore* me with gory stories about your latest cramps or your incredible labor pains or how many times your hubby bangs you every week."

That was the last thing I'd bore anybody with. But now I've blown it.

"Why do you ask?"

See, she is suspicious. She gets up and pads across the room in her bare feet to the wine decanter.

"You drink too much," I tell her. I am drinking coffee.

"It's five-thirty," she says, returning with a glass for me too. "Got to steady my nerves for the onslaught. I've got three more hours to go before Buddy-boy pulls in here. Shit! Kate Millett makes more sense to me than anything I've read since Karl Marx. I'm telling you, you ought to read her."

She sits on the floor next to me.

"Now!" she says, scaring me. "Girl talk. Have I ever had a lover? Have *you* ever had a lover? That's what I want to know."

"No."

"You've got one now?"

"No."

"You're thinking of getting one?"

Like I'd *get* a new couch or a new washing machine. "No. What's *wrong* with you?"

"Then why did you ask? You're not keeping anything from Cousin Connie, are you? Because I got the strangest feeling about you when I called this morning. The way you picked up the phone and said 'Good Morning!', just as if you were expecting someone."

Telepathy is not the most precise of sciences. "I just wondered. It popped into my head when you mentioned Billy Butler. Wasn't he married in college and going with someone on the side?"

"How am I supposed to remember anything about that hophead fifteen years ago? Listen, Lily. I'm having an affair right now, and I feel just dandy."

Oh. She's my best friend.

"I'm sorry. You're shocked, aren't you?"

"Yes." I am.

"I'm sorry."

"You didn't *tell* me." How could you? Think of Bud.

"I couldn't. You're such a morality nut."

"I'm sorry."

"You are, you know."

"I know. I'm sorry." I keep saying that. "I'll recover," I say. "I know how it must be with Bud away so much."

"It's not only Bud. It's the whole society."

"Please, Connie. Not today. Not the spiel."

"You gripe about being behind the times. That's just a euphemism for being repressed. Unliberated. A prisoner of sex."

"My gripe is merely that I haven't got anything to do all day except sit around and polish the silver." But *you*. Look what *you're* doing, Connie, my Connie.

"That's the whole point. You *had* a great job. You've been shat upon."

"I've got to go." I get up off the floor. "I'll call you."

"You're disgusted with me, aren't you?"

"No. It's your life."

She helps me on with my jacket, an unusual tenderness for her. "I'm sorry I reacted the way I did," I say. "I shouldn't judge." Her eyes fill with tears.

"It's serious?"

"I don't know," she says. "I'm a damned fool."

We gather up hats and scarves and go outside to collect trucks and a football, and I lure the boys into the car with promises of food. She leans in the car window on the far side. "Call me," she says.

"I will." I won't.

"I'll tell you about George." Unrepentant.

"Couldn't he at least have been a Clarke or a Craig or a Clarence?"

"George Raft," she says, "George Hamilton. George Harrison. What's wrong with that?"

"George Allen. George Burns. George Washington."

She laughs. Gay. Happy. Adulteress. Why can't *I?*

59

I start the car and back down her long rhododendron-bordered driveway. Ian, I think. I'll never tell a soul about you.

I drive home over hilly winding roads. The sky seen from the hilltops is still bright with day, but evening has already come to the houses in the dips and hollows of the hills. The boys are tired after an afternoon of roughhouse and suck quietly at their thumbs in the back seat as we speed over the familiar road. On the radio Simon and Garfunkel sing *Like a bridge over troubled waters I will lay me down.* Who will I lay me down for?

I know I will not call her. I don't want to hear about "George." "Are we having an affair?" Ian wrote this week. "What will happen when we see each other again? Will we make love?" All questions that are eating at the edges of the block of consciousness in my own head labeled Ian. What is going to happen?

The memory of his long athlete's body as I had seen it on the beach inflames my mind when I let myself travel over it in my secret depths. I hanker for him and lie awake at night to dwell in solitude on him. I call up his broad face, his large head of light and clean hair that falls floppily away on both sides of a part set low down on the left side of his head. His eyebrows are dark and low, too, and ride on the ridge of his gray eyes, which consequently seem to be forever peering at one as if from out of a cave. The caveman cast, which I have come to be fond of, as a mother can grow to be fond of, say, her child's cross-eyed-ness, is heightened by a slight Neanderthal forward stoop to his walk. Sometimes, of course, I wonder if this characterization is wishful thinking—this fantasizing of mine that he is some kind of caveman who will come one day to drag me away from my other man. It would be so convenient if he were, wouldn't it? *My* will would not be in question. *I* would have to have no guilt at going with him.

He has a mouth that is a *mouth*, almost a woman's mouth, in fact, so perfectly etched and symmetrical that a woman would be lucky to have it, and a nose that looks as if it has been bashed by a brickbat, or a club.

He is not at all a "handsome" man. If he were I would have steered clear of him. Such men make me uneasy; they are always better-looking than I. But he has the pleasantest face, the nicest, most comfortable mannish man's face, despite his woman's mouth, that ever looked at me. It is engraved in the air around me. I see it everywhere.

"I love you," he wrote yesterday, and the sight of the words shot an arrow of desire into my center so sharp I felt pain. *Like a bridge over troubled waters, I will ease your mind.* Jonas: come home and ease my mind.

Adultery. I don't like that word. After reading the letter in which he first put my fantasy into his own words, Will we make love, I tore it into pieces, put the pieces in a paper lunchbag, twisted the lunchbag with an energy that would make one think there was some vile wound of a sandwich inside, and threw it into the trash can.

But this reaction was merely an initial one, and it went away, because he has guaranteed me from the start, hasn't he, a courtesy or distance, an option to decide for myself what I will do that disarms me when I feel myself pursued? Hasn't there been a mental quality there from the start, an engagement of our spirits that preceded any crude question of a physical engagement, a trust we share that lets me consider that question now with equanimity?

Yes. Almost. Almost. As I cross the lawn from garage

to house, Teddy at my heels and Peter in my arms, half asleep, his little towhead on my shoulder, his hand covering my breast, the only equanimity I feel now is that which comes from doing right.

I put Ian out of my mind and settle the boys down on the couch in the kitchen to color and look at books while I bring the house to life with lights and music, and simmer our dinner—chicken legs, carrots, potatoes, and an onion in an orange saucepan on the stove. My children, my warm savory kitchen, my sturdy house, my glass of sherry, my husband, my Little King, winging homeward to me in the morning, these give me equanimity and the only peace of mind I can ever know. Ian is going to destroy it all.

8

J ONAS comes home during the night, smelling like airplane fuel, and desirous. I gratify him. Thinking of Ian all the while.

In the morning he is astonished to see what I have done. "I don't like this at all," he says angrily. "This isn't Hampton Court, and you're not Anne Boleyn. I want this taken down."

"I'm not going to take it down."

"It looks lousy. I don't want it backed up to the house like that. We have enough drainage problems here as it is."

"Don't be ridiculous. The back wall *is* the house. Nothing new is backed *up* to it."

He turns and struts quickly into the house.

I follow him in.

"Where are the boys?" He has slept late, after his travels.

"Why do you always have to come home mad?"

"Where are they?"

"They go to the Y on Saturday mornings for gymnast class."

"I thought they'd be here when I got home."

"They *were* here, dear. They were asleep. It was late, remember?"

"I want to see them."

"I didn't even tell them you were here. They wouldn't have wanted to go to class if they'd known. And I wanted you to myself this morning. I missed you." I stroke his unshaved cheek. "I *missed* you." I *did* miss him.

I have disarmed him. He takes my hand and holds it in his lap. "I don't like that thing you built, Lily," he says plaintively. He looks very tired and down. Traveling takes a lot out of him.

"I know."

"What are you going to do about it?"

"I'm going to leave it there." I speak with perfect gravity.

"I never thought you'd do a thing like this to me, Lily. Why, you've practically added a whole room onto the house without even asking me. You've changed my house. My property."

"The mason said I did a fantastic job. The lines are nice and straight. It was a labor of love, Jonas. It took me two weeks." Whose love.

"I'm coming down with an awful cold, Lily. I feel it coming on. You're just making me feel worse by arguing with me."

"I'm sorry. Shall I make you some tea?"

"Won't you take it down?" he asks, sipping his tea a little later.

"No."

"Lily, it's so *unlike* you to go against me."

"Jonas. You are *boring* me. I am not going to take it down. It's mine. I made it. And I love it." Jonas and I never fight. We only speak in italics.

"Please?"

"Oh, stop making such a fuss about it." I tell him how it will be when the pear tree blooms and starts to espalier and how the roses are going to be the palest most delicate shade of pink in the world. He is a pushover for pink. "It's going to *enhance* your property."

He glares at me, discouraged. "I don't know what's gotten *into* you," he says.

9

AN opportunity to work again presents itself in May. Mr. D'Allessandro needs me to prepare a catalog for a special exhibit the library is having in the fall. The new assistant curator is as incompetent as the two before him, to my tiny gratification.

The prospect of getting back to the serene yet busy atmosphere of the library, even if only for a few weeks, makes me very happy. Jonas is pleased, too. He sees it as an opportunity to commute together, to have lunch together one day, and maybe even to stay in one night to "paint the town red," as he puts it. "The boys won't suffer for a week or two," he concludes.

"I don't care if they do," I say. "I suffer enough for them." He looks at me.

I think he secretly hopes the commute will do me in, make me forget once and for all about the subversive idea of working.

Mr. D'Allessandro is waiting at Grand Central Station the first morning to meet my train! I feel like a child again —a tall schoolgirl in for a vacation treat with her favorite uncle.

He is a tiny little man with a silky goatee on his chin, to make up, I think, for what is missing on the top of his head. I feel so big and brawny next to him that I imagine I could pick him up and carry him down Park Avenue in my arms, like a baby. "Leely!" he squeaks. "Leely. My tall Leely of the field. You have come back to me!" If I got down on my knees he could throw his arms around my neck.

"Mr. Dallie," I croak. "I have returned."

"You are more beautiful than ever, my flower. You have a special beauty. There is something happy in your life, yes?"

"Oh, yes!" I bend and bob. "My life is very agreeable these days. And I'm so happy to be working again."

"Ah, we will make a beautiful catalog together, Leely. We will get everything just right. Yes?"

"Yes! No bloopers this time."

"Bloopers! That word bloopers! That means the same as boo-boos. Yes? The last one. Leely, he made so many boo-boos. Nothing up here." He taps his forehead.

He prances along beside me as I stride to the library. I am so eager to get back. Even Ian is eclipsed today.

May softens the city with green and gold. The sky is high and blue and the air seems clean. A good New York day. Nothing in the world like it. Privet glistens at the front stoops of brownstones, and hawthorn blooms in the library courtyard. But I hardly stop to notice. I am quivering to get at my chores.

The library is unchanged, the same solemn stillness, the same strips of sun falling on the same parquets, the same marble bathrooms and, on the paneled walls, the same framed faces forever frowning. And on the first day when I go out to walk at noon to see the neighborhood, I find that it has not changed either. They have not torn down any buildings and put up any new ones in my absence, the same family still owns the same delicatessen, the same department store is doing the same business, the same church is still having its same unattended noontime services. Only people's looks have changed. There is something in the air. It is hair. Everyone is growing it. And it is breasts. Women by the dozens have liberated their breasts. I am very taken aback by this, but also, after the first shock has passed, very interested in it. It seems to me such an intrepid thing to do, so fine and bold and wicked, something I do not think I could ever do.

I watch the faces of the men around me to see what they think about it, but hardly a flicker of interest lights their eyes. I stand at the corner of Madison Avenue and watch, and I am the only one seemingly at all aware of the phenomenon. A harried girl wearing jeans and an orange sweater housing a beautiful unfettered bosom waits near me next to a suitcase. Her boyfriend approaches. Her face relaxes at the sight of him and her breasts, miraculously, stand up. I am mortified for her, yet fascinated.

"I hope you remembered to pack my tennis shoes," he says. Not even hello. Not even thank you for those beautiful boobies. I wonder at him.

When I turn back down the avenue toward the library, I catch a glimpse of myself in a plate-glass window. The whole configuration of me is all wrong! I am too carefully mixed and matched, a suburban woman in town for lunch and a matinee. Yet I move, I think, with a certain floating grace that suggests there is more to me than meets the eye. There are possibilities here. Unrealized, perhaps, but here. I take off my boater and place it in a large aluminum-mesh trash basket that handily appears, and glide on up the block, pausing to look back only when I am a safe distance away. It has been chosen by a stout woman in red, and she is admiring herself in it in front of a shop window. I hope she is happy with it.

That evening when I sink into the seat beside Jonas on the 5:38 I am in total disarray. I have run four blocks to make the train, carrying my coat, the *Times,* and a large manila envelope full of papers that I have promised Mr. D'Allessandro I will read before tomorrow. I have run my stockings. My lipstick has long since worn off, my hair is tangled, my fingers are stained with ink. I am exhausted. But I feel full of myself and good.

"See," Jonas says. "And you want to do this every day."

"If I did it every day, it would be a lot easier." I am panting. It will take me to Riverdale to catch my breath.

He smiles a secret smile and bends to the stock prices. "What are we having for dinner?" he asks as the train lurches out of the station.

"Meat loaf."

He smiles again. "Well, I suppose you working women have to compromise somewhere."

"Shut up, Jonas," I say. "You love meat loaf."

He chuckles and returns to his paper.

By the time we get home it is almost 7:30. The boys are wild to see me. They nearly knock me over.

As soon as he leaves to take the sitter home, I rush to look at the mail. There is a letter. I slip it behind the toaster and set the table. We eat our overcrisp meat loaf and baked potatoes and canned tomatoes in the kitchen, with the boys clamoring around us for our attention.

"Mommy, Mommy, I learned to tie my shoes today," Teddy shouts.

"Can you tie them now, Teddy?" asks little Peter, full of wonder at his big brother.

69

"No," says Teddy sadly.

"That's O.K.," says Peter. "You can learn again."

We tie Teddy's shoes several times to show him how he did it, but he claims we are doing it wrong. He is angry with us now, with me, for having left him all day.

"I made a gun, Mommy," Peter shouts. "Want to see my gun?" He produces two pieces of wood nailed together in an L-shape with many, many nails. "That's *nice*, Peter." I am so proud of him. "Did you do that all by yourself?" He beams. Jonas examines it conscientiously too.

"That's not a gun," says Teddy. "It doesn't shoot."

Peter shoots him and they race off rat-a-tat-tatting through the house.

"I went to Philadelphia today," says Jonas, shoving his plate away.

I am surprised. "Why?" I give him a bowl of ice cream.

"There was a selling situation involving the conservatory and whether they would buy three of our eight-and-a-half-footers or three of somebody else's. Anderson let us down again, so the manager of the store called at nine this morning and asked me to come down to help him out. I took the ten o'clock train. They're going to order from us." He is very pleased with himself.

"I'm so *proud* of you, dear. Why didn't you tell me on the train?"

"I was mad at you."

"For working?"

"Yes."

"Jonas."

"I hate to see you looking so fagged."

"It's only the first day."

"It's a long day, no matter what day it is."

"What are you going to do about Anderson?" The regional manager for the mid-central region.

"Fire him."

"Who's going to replace him?"

"I'd like to see Ian come up."

I knew he was going to say that, but my blood rushes anyway. I start to stack the dishes in the dishwasher. And then he adds, "But first I'll give him one more chance." Someday he will say that about me. Jonas is just. Always just. He will give you many chances. But he has *his* frustration level too. And then there are no more chances.

We put the boys to bed, and I take a hot bath with the door locked and Ian in the tub with me—that part of him that is in the letter.

He is coming!

I do cartwheels all over the ceiling. I go underwater like a happy seal. I throw bubbles in the air to catch on my nose. He is coming! They are driving to Pittsburgh to visit Becky's mother for a week in the middle of June. "Will you be at home?" he asks. "Can I see you? I can say I have to go to New York to see Jonas for a few days in the middle of the week."

All of me, why not see all of me, I sing to the echo in the big bathroom. But later, when I am in bed next to slumbering Jonas, I do not feel quite so gay. My play world is coming to an end. I am going to deceive my Little King for real.

10

AT five I rise to clear the dishwasher, run a load of laundry, and write to Ian. "I am afraid to see you. I am afraid of what we are going to do. But come. Come anyway. You can stay in the apartment over our garage. Nobody ever goes up there. Darling, do you know I feel angry that you are coming? But I want you to anyway? I am so mixed up about it all."

What am I doing, I think. What *am* I doing? He can't stay here. I mail the letter from Grand Central, after kissing Jonas good-bye.

I go at noon to a beauty salon for a consultation. My consultant, stretching a pink uniform, studies me frontways and sideways. I study her from the tassels on her white vinyl boots to the top of her shiny black wig. She is wearing a bra. "You're out of date," she says. "You're just out of date."

I've always been that. I'm sure it can be remedied. "Is it my hair?"

"It's partly your hair. But we can fix you up with a new hairdo. Give you today's Look. You want to say, I like sex. See? The sensuous woman. That's the look today."

I look at myself in the mirror. Actually, I don't see how she is going to change me. I have looked one way nearly all my life.

"And that lipstick, honey," she is saying. "That's got to go. Orange hasn't been around for years. And if you're really serious, you'll get yourself some new clothes."

I look down at my good Saks suit that I have had for three or four years. I know something is wrong with it, but I am not sure what. "What is there about this that's wrong?" I ask her.

"It's just Out of Date," she says in capital letters. "The Look is wrong. Go over to Alexander's and see what the kids are wearing."

"But I'm thirty-four."

"I'm forty-two. Look how good I look," she says.

I don't think she looks so good, but I make a note in my head about Alexander's and leave with twenty-one dollars' worth of makeup and night creams and wake-up rinses. She makes an appointment for me to have my hair "styled."

I meet Jonas on the train again and describe the contents of all my new little jars and pots and how they will make me beautiful and up-to-date. "But I like you the way you are," he says. "And I like your hair. Don't change it."

I look at myself in the dark train window as we move through the tunnel.

My eyes look back at me from under a blond fringe of shiny hair that just clears my eyebrows. The rest of my hair is tucked behind my ears, convenient hooks to keep it out of my way. My eyes are gray and darting, like a bird's; the pupils are tiny now, in the lights of the train, but they grow large and soft and black after love in a darkened room. My nose is long and sharp and contends with my cheekbones for prominence. Only my mouth is neither sharp nor darting. It is curving and full and soft and redeems the angularity of the rest of me. I like me. Jonas likes me. Ian likes me. Why should I change?

At home, I experiment in my room with the makeup, at first making a whore's face without meaning to. I wash it off and try again. Finally, I go downstairs and sit in the living room where Jonas is watching television. He looks at me, but doesn't see me. I study the woman who is singing to us on the screen. She is beautiful and tarty at the same time. I like her. When the program is over, we sit at the kitchen table and have a cup of tea. After a while, he says, "Is that the makeup?"

"Yes. Do you like it?"

"Not really."

I don't like it either. It feels heavy and hot. Before going to bed I try again. This time I leave off the foundation cream and the sunnyrose liquid color stuff and the blusher and the eyeliner, the mascara and the eyeshadow, and try with only the new lipstick and the rouge, and I get it just right. I love my new mauve mouth. "Do I look beautiful and tarty, Jonas?"

"Yes," he says. He is sitting on the edge of the bed in his underwear, clipping his toenails into the wastebasket. "How about it tonight?"

"Not tonight," I say, loving my face in a hand mirror. Lily, you are something else yourself. Tall me, floppy bangs, long fine eyebrows lengthening out on one side to a mole high on my temple, growing tenderly together in the middle. Dark-lashed eagle eyes, long lip deeply furrowed, curving mouth now frosted mauve. You are getting there, my dear.

"Got a boyfriend?"

"Yes." I pull my hair forward and let it fall around my face so that I look like a medieval page. It suits me, especially now that I have offered a bed in my barn to Launcelot. He whacks me on the rear end as he walks past me to go to the bathroom. "Let's take a shower."

That means we'll do it.

What's wrong with that?

We clasp each other under the spray and rock back and forth. "I love you," he says. "I love you, too, Jonas; I really do." He wants to in the shower, but I skit away from him and soap him down instead. "In New York I feel so out of it; my looks."

"I know what you mean," he says. "I need a new image, too. Got to get groovy."

"Oh, groovy. I hate that word."

"That's your trouble," he says. "You don't want to get with it."

In bed we make love quickly. I have so many things on my mind that at first I don't even care how it is. But then, despite myself, I do. It is very nice, and we lie calmly together afterward. I am happy, content. But, then, why am I doing what I am doing? I start to weep, and he holds me closer, stroking my back. "Jonas," I cry, "don't let me go."

"I'll never do that," he says.

"I'm so afraid."

"Of what?" He is perplexed by me once again.

"That I'll run away from you." I sob. I don't want ever to leave this man, this anchor of mine.

"You won't run away. I won't let you. We're stuck with each other." He rocks me.

"I'm going to feel so trapped again when this job is over."

"I know."

"If only I could *do* something. If only I could *be* somebody."

"You are. You are."

"It isn't enough. I have nothing. I'm not anybody," I whisper and whisper.

He holds me and strokes my hair. "You have everything," he says. "I love you. You're my woman. The time will come, I promise, Lily. It will come."

"But how, when?"

"Shhh. We'll think of something. Papa will fix it."

"I just want you to know," I say fiercely. "I just want you to know, I *mind* spending my whole life waiting on your little messiahs."

"Don't get ugly," he says sharply, loosening my grip on his arm. "I know. So let's go to sleep. We'll think of something one of these days."

Jonas sleeps. I lie awake thinking of my life. He is right and wise, of course, in seeing what we have together, everything there is to have: our health, our boys, our love, our house, our sufficient income—everything, that is, but my contentment. We no longer have that. So Jonas is wrong in thinking I will never leave him. I may well go away.

He has satisfied the need I had to be led into the confidence I lacked. But now I have that, and I am needing a man who will let me expand and express myself in the adult way I have avoided till now. I dimly realize that something is wrong with this. Why should I need a *man* to let me do it? But if not a man, who then? What then?

To Jonas, I think I will always be the spoiled only child he married, but being the little girl of the family no longer appeals to me.

Ian has come along at a time when something besides the little girl in me wants to be expressed, perhaps only a new ripened sensuality. But perhaps something more than that, too: a new awareness of time passing and of fleeting change of which I have been no part, a new faith in myself that wants to try itself in the world, and a new notion that there is something to which I am better suited than the keeping of house in a house that is empty all day. All the other things I have and am are not enough, because now it tantalizes me not to be those things any more than I have been all my thirty-four years: not to be a dutiful daughter, not to be a child-wife, not to be a slave mother, not to be a keeper of my word.

Jonas circumscribes the world he chose for me to live in. He has made me what it suits him to have his woman be. Ian is the lever I can pull to catapult myself out of that world. But into one I am not at all sure I want to be in either.

That is the trouble. What *is* Ian? And what is Ian's world?

I roam down the moonlit stairs and sink into an armchair in the living room, the shapes of the furniture familiar as family around me.

Jonas has given me the life I once thought I wanted, of genial family-making and of comfort. But Ian has engaged me in a way so singular, so uncommon, that if I pass it up it will never come to me again. And that is something I have always wanted too.

He has affected my very soul. I will never know the likes of it again.

And so, I think, I have to have you, Ian, as much of you as I can take.

But that is a perilous thing to say, and as soon as I have said it I feel unreal and removed from myself, suspended above myself, dangling precariously from an enormous helium balloon that is about to carry me off into a foreign country from which I will never return. I shudder, to dispel the thought. And try to bind myself to earth with particulars.

What am I to Ian? How does he see me? I think I am

special, a treasure only he has been able to discover—that only he has sensed was there to discover. You have an aura, my Laura, he writes, that quiets you and secrets you and removes you from what is around you. You move set apart from the rest of us, and I set myself apart from them to go to you. Your eyes call me. Can we, Lily, in another time and place live our love?

Can we, Ian? How would we start? Where would we begin? Whose state would we live in? Whose children would we have? Whose money would we spend? Whose love would we lose? Whose love are we free to lose?

Did we walk along the empty beach together, Ian, the tiny surf that day curling up through our toes, licking our ankles with wet tongues of spray, sun ripening our backs?

Did we lie in the gentle surge, letting the motion drag us out and float us in and drag us out and float us in again, our toes and fingers and once our bellies meeting in tiny kisses, your hair spreading around you in the water, your face intent on mine? Did we let finally the surge of surf place us on the sand so we could do in the warm deeps of me what it is we want to do, think we are meant to do? Oh, Ian. I don't know if we did or not. I can't tell what we did from what I've dreamed we've done.

Ian, you think that I am my own woman, wise and calm, strong and resourceful. But you are wrong, my love. I am not that. I am not that yet. I only appear to be that. In reality I am Jonas's woman, merely. An appendage to Jonas's existence. It is through you that I am somehow going to become what you think I am.

You imagine that I would enhance your mean life, let your being have its say again. And about that you *are* right. Your being would have its say in the house I make for you with all the beauties that you covet: a down sofa to love on, hand-woven flax of softest blue at our windows, pink earthen pots uneven as melons to hold our flowers, and a Persian rug to lie on before a well-used hearth. Does Becky let you love in the living room, Ian?

I touch the fabric of the chair I sit in and caress it as if it were his skin. You see in me, Ian, a force and energy to change your life, to mention only that, that I did not know I had. I am delighted to know it. And I am angry at Jonas for not imagining that I had it. And I am surprised at myself for allowing him not to imagine it.

Jonas is wrong. Wifing and mothering are necessary, but they are not sufficient. I want more. Ian tells me I can have more. Jonas thinks more would be bad for me, bad for him. I am trapped in his dream of how it should be. I have had to give up my own. But now I have a new dream, and I am not going to give it up. So listen to me.

I have the dream that I can live in two worlds, and pay no price for my dual citizenship.

Or is it too much to ask, this schizoid fantasy that I have quilted out of the stuff of my nothingness?

Of course it is. I know that. A dreamy fantasy world, and with impunity, with no pain to bear for the deserting, is too much to ask. I know that. So why should I put the question? Choices are given to be made.

11

AT the outdoor cafe I select a table at the rear and order an iced tea, which I sip slowly while I wait for Claudine. The drink is unpleasant—neither iced nor tea. It has a strange warm thickness to it, and a syrupy sweet taste. Even the small dice-shaped ice cubes seem unnatural to me.

Madison Avenue swarms with New Yorkers strolling in the noon sun. I find them bizarre. I am of another time and tempo, and it exhausts me just to look at them in their loony get-ups.

"I'm sorry I'm late. It's impossible to make any headway in this crowd. You look divine, Puss! Haven't changed a hair!" She flings herself down at the table, scattering menus and forks and claiming a chair from an adjacent table for her parcels and handbag. She is in a patchwork of beige and pink suede, her blond hair to her waist, her breasts perky through her pongee blouse.

"Claudine! *You* have."

"You haven't seen me in three years, m'dear. Iced tea? How can you drink that swill? I'll have a martini, please. Very dry up with a twist."

"Has it been three years?" I am appalled. At her. What can I say to this creature I once knew so well?

"Or more. You were big as a house with one of your babbies. Remember? Huffing and puffing. You could hardly make it back to your train." She laughs merrily at this image of me.

"It's four years then. That was Peter."

"Peter. So you have two *petit fils*. I always forget. We career women you know. Can't keep up with you breeders in the boondocks."

"Well," I say, "as I recall, your career wasn't exactly flourishing four years ago. Weren't you on welfare? I do remember paying for your lunch."

"Collecting unemployment. Not quite the same thing. Don't you want a drink?" She orders another martini and a Jell-o salad plate. (Jell-o: sugar, gelatin, adipic acid, sodium citrate, fumaric acid, artificial colors and flavors.) I order a grilled Swiss cheese on whole wheat and a glass of skimmed milk.

"Seriously, Lily, you do look grand. That country air must do something for you. Easier on your skin, anyway."

Hers is concealed under makeup. But she is still pretty, I suppose, by modern standards. I ask her if she is wearing a bra.

"Not much of one. Like me?" She looks down at herself.

I must admit I do. But what about the men in her office. Isn't it rather diverting for them?

"That's the point, dumdum," she says. "Unfortunately, it's been so overdone they don't even notice any more."

"I thought maybe it had some political significance."

"Balls."

To me, she is all wrong. I find her monstrous, with her tough hip talk and her avid eyes and her indecent exposure and her long pink-blond hair that wants to make men think of her in nothing else. I don't know what to talk about to her. We are worlds apart. "Are you still in publishing?"

"No. Too draggy for me. I'm a copywriter for an ad agency." She is bored with me and my square talk. But, of course, we will see it through.

"And Elliott?" I have never met him, her second husband.

"Elliott?" Her face is so blank that I think for a moment I have the wrong name. "He's a lawyer, didn't you know?"

"I forgot."

"Don't ever marry one. They're work-freaks. Washouts as husbands." She nibbles on a cracker, one eye on the parade going by on the sidewalk. "How about Jonas? How's he turning out?"

"He's good. I like him. We're happy." Yes, all those things are true.

"Well, I can't say the same. But I compensate."

"Oh. You have a lover."

"A friend."

Do I have a lover? I don't know. I think of Ian, warm, urgent, excitable, his lips passing over mine in Georgia, his letters full of warnings of what not to eat. He loves me. He wants me to eat right. I feel in my pocket for a pignolia nut from the store he sent me. My boys love his figs. They love his Granola. But is he my lover? Is he going to be? Oh, Ian. I remember that I must stop at the health-food store on the way back to the library. We are out of organic peanut butter.

"Well, if it isn't Claudine and Miss Lily."

"Go blow, Howard," says Claudine, so quick on the draw.

"Hello, Howard," I say coldly. "Good-bye, Howard."

He pulls up a chair and makes himself at home. "Now is that nice? I thought they taught you Barnard girls better manners than that."

"Just our luck," says Claudine. "We get to see each other once in four years, and this idiot has to butt in."

"Now, now," he says, picking up the pickle from my plate and popping it into his mouth. "Anything you girls have to say you can say in front of unshockable Uncle Howie. Talking about your boyfriends, weren't you?" He masticates, his red rubbery mouth working over my gherkin.

"Howie, get lost, will you." She snatches her pack of cigarettes back from him. He has been married to two girls we know—for a few months, it was said, to both of them at the same time.

"Look at Claudine's boobies, everybody. Ain't they cute?"

She tries to stub her cigarette out on the back of his hand, but he is quicker and chops her wrist down.

"Let's go, Lily. We won't be able to get rid of him."

"We have to get the check." I am ready. I detest this creep.

She jumps up to look for our waitress. He grins, uncertainly now. I shake my head at him. "When are you ever going to start being a good boy?"

"I'm sorry, Miss Lily. If I had you to teach me. Why don't you come over to my place this afternoon? You know what we could do?"

"You're impossible." I gather my things.

"The sex revolution passed you right by, didn't it, Lily?" he hisses. And then louder, as I start to stand up and walk away: "What've you got on under that shirtdress? Lollypop pants and a Maidenform bra?"

People look at me as I flee. How did he know?

We pay and leave him there, scanning the crowd with his busy, busy eyes.

We tell each other how sorry we are that it happened that way, how good it was to see each other again, how we must get together again very soon for a good talk, how we must get our men together. I have a quick mental picture of Jonas and Elliott bowing to her lover and mine while kimonoed she and I pass tea in porcelain bowls in the background. Ah, so.

We say good-bye many times at the light on the corner and are ever so glad to leave tedious one another. I notice two men watching us. I wonder what they are thinking about us, her in her leather skirt, her sandals laced to the thigh, her long hair swinging come get me, and me in my gray and white Marimekko with its full skirt and little-girl sash. I know what they think. They think we are so different. But who is to say. We are both cheating. The difference is that I am doing it in secret.

12

I AM glad when Jonas calls and suggests that we meet tonight in the bar car, even though I know he is only being kind to me because he is going to California on Monday for two weeks.

I can hardly bear to think what it will be like, with him gone and me working and the boys not liking the babysitter I have hired. I would like to fire her and ask my mother to help me for two weeks, but I am saving her patience for June, when Ian comes. I plan to take the boys to her that week, to let us be.

Jonas is jolly, but I am not taken in. We will speak in italics before the weekend is over. I want to make sure he knows how I hate it when he goes away, leaving me to do everything and not even having the comfort of him in the house at night. He keeps bringing up our vacation, as if to remind me that we will all be together as I like it in just another month. But before we go, Jonas, do you have any idea what is going to happen to you? I picture him innocently giraffe-like, a little pair of soft spotted horns growing out of his forehead. He touches the curious excrescences, as if to say, What could they *be?*

We sip our Scotch slowly, to make it last. We don't like the idea of going home smashed to the boys. But we have a second drink anyway. It is too long a trip for just one.

Mrs. Bush's well-loathed form waits outside by the back steps. She is wearing her sweater and hat; her handbag is at the ready. I make her wait a little longer while I write out her check for the week. Sixty hours equals one hundred and twenty dollars. Almost all of my take-home pay and not tax deductible either. And I had to pay the cleaning woman twenty dollars for Wednesday. It's a good thing I don't have to support myself.

I notice that the boys don't say good-bye to Bush when Jonas takes her home. Peter says she has whiskers when I ask him how she was with him today. Teddy says she stinks.

I think she stinks too when I go into the house and see the way she has left it. I have been getting up at half-past five all week in order to get it straightened before I leave. When Jonas comes in with her at 7:15, the beds are made, the kitchen floor swept, the counters cleared, the rooms picked up, the dishwasher rattling busily. Yet she has left this day's dishes food-clotted in the sink and not even bothered to unload yesterday's from the machine.

I slip french fries and two frozen lobster tails into the oven and set some butter to melt on the top of the stove while I wash a head of Boston lettuce and lay our silver on the table. The day's debris is all over the house that was so orderly when I left it this morning. "She used our Tiffany glasses for the boys," I fume when Jonas returns. "She was too damned lazy to take the everyday ones out of the machine, or to wash out the ones she used this morning. Look!"

He is upset by my being upset and also because he does not like the woman. "There's something about her," he

86

says. "She looks like someone I saw once in the *Daily News* who committed an ax murder."

"Please!" I shudder to think I may have left my sons, my blond treasures, in the hands of an assassin. We eat unhappily in silence. I do not know what to do.

That night as we undress the boys for bed, I notice four little blue marks high on Peter's left arm. "What this?"

"Mrs. Bush squeezed me," he says, looking at the little bruises.

"Why?"

"I wouldn't stand in the corner."

"Why did she want you to stand in the corner?"

"I wouldn't eat my lunch."

I snap his top to his bottoms. "And what happened after she squeezed you?"

"I cried."

"And what else?"

"Teddy socked her."

"And then what did she do to Teddy?"

"She punched him back on his head."

"She won't be coming here ever again," I tell him. "You don't have to worry. We won't let her come here any more, ever."

Teddy corroborates the story. "She socked me so hard on my ear that I fell down, Mom," he says seriously.

Jonas is wild, and I am beside myself. He calls her on the phone and threatens to have her arrested. "Those are vicious children you have," she screams. "That big one punched me in the stomach."

"If I ever see you again, I'll punch you in the stomach, too," I hear Jonas shout. And he hangs up on her.

"I didn't like her from the beginning," he says, storming into the kitchen.

I didn't either, but now what am I going to do?

I call Connie to tell her. She gives me the names of a few sitters she has used. She is sympathetic and helpful, as her ideologists suggest she should be when a sister is in trouble. I ask them to come over on Sunday afternoon for a drink and a cookout, and then I start calling the women and setting up interviews for the morning. I am exhausted. I think of myself as having been bushwhacked by a Bush whack.

Jonas, who has been making listening noises all this time, crossing his legs, shaking his newspaper, sighing and clearing his throat, finally comes out to the kitchen again and says what is on his mind. He doesn't like the idea of getting someone else. He thinks I should call Mr. D'Allessandro and tell him I can't go back on Monday.

"But they're not all like her," I protest. "She was just a nut." I have to go to work. I have to. But he looks very sour.

Finally, he says, "Look. I'll cancel my trip and stay home for two weeks while you finish the catalog, if it's that important to you."

It would really be very dear of him, if it were not so insincere. He knows I wouldn't let him do that. "I won't leave them if I don't have complete confidence in the next woman," I promise him.

"Didn't you have complete confidence in Bush?"

"Not really."

"Well?"

"She wasn't referred. I got her from an ad in the paper. The ones tomorrow have all worked for people we know."

"Frankly," he says, "Connie is not my idea of the super-careful mother. I wish you'd change your mind."

"Jonas, I have a thing about disappointing people."

"You don't seem to have a 'thing' about disappointing

me. I guess I'm not important around here. I'm only the poor slob who pays all the bills for this . . . this . . . *estate* we have here."

It was his idea to buy it. I didn't want to live way up here. But I say nothing, having learned long ago not to fuel his empty ravings.

"You don't even seem to be bothered about the boys," he goes on, warming to the battle. "All you care about is yourself, and that little shortcut to nothing you work for." And Ian. Don't forget him. I care about him. But I set the table for breakfast and keep still.

"Will you change your mind then?"

"No."

"You're going to risk the boys' lives, then, is that it?"

"No. You're ex*agg*erating. I promise you it won't happen again."

"You *promise?* Ha!"

I hate him when he sneers. I go in and sit down on the couch in the living room and pick up a magazine. He follows me. Stands in front of me. His will against mine. "You mean you won't change your mind?"

"No, I won't, Jonas."

"All right," he says coldly. "I hold you responsible."

I go up miserably to bed.

Saturday, between interviews, I make beds, pick up toys and clothes, vacuum rugs, do laundry, prepare meals, pay bills, go to the supermarket for a week's worth of groceries. By the end of the afternoon, I have hired a new woman.

She is clearly not an ax murderer. She wears a crisp white jabot at her throat and Enna Jetticks and asks if she may stay for an hour to let the boys get used to her. Even Jonas agrees that she is admirable.

But I am spent, my resources flushed out of me in the

89

labor of choosing her, in the strife with him, in the Ian-guilt that enfolds me now like a fog, in the fright it gives me to think of the chances I have taken with my happiness, in the physical work I have had to do on top of it all. It is all too much for me, and so I tell him not to come, and go to bed at nine o'clock fearing only the consequences of the last chance I will take, that Jonas will see the red flag up on the mailbox in the morning before the letter to Savan-nah is removed.

This thought disturbs me so that it wakes me at dawn, and I creep out of the sleeping house and go noiselessly in the June sunrise on my bike to the village and leave my last word there and then go home to sit in my garden and ache for him and for what I haven't known.

The first roses of the season are of palest pink and yellow and as big as melons, and the dew sparkling down through the sunny verdant acres to the woods recalls the morning grace we sang at summer camp years ago, something about summer mornings being silver and green and gold. I can almost hear girlish voices rising in the green, sun-dappled woods and see the silver lake shining down the hill from the open-air dining hall, and I think how simple life was then, and how complicated I have made it. But I have reversed that now, and we are safe again; we are together. It matters not at all that in all these years of marriage I have let one man not Jonas kiss my mouth.

But still I ache and keen, and Jonas sees it in my face an hour later and thinks it is because he is going away, or because I am worried about leaving the boys again on Mon-day. He puts his arms around me as I turn the bacon, and I weep bitterly. Oh, Ian. I wanted you so. You were meant for me, dearest brightness.

"Just two more weeks," he soothes. "And I'll be back

and your job will be over, and then school will end and we can start packing to go."

Yes, all that is so. And the job *is* too much for me. Nothing is worth sixty hours a week. But why couldn't I have met Ian instead of Jonas? Why can't I have you both, now that I know you exist, my Ian? I dry my eyes on the tie of his bathrobe and turn the bacon again.

"How about trying to find a little part-time job around here?"

He says it as if the idea has just popped into his head for the first time. But I have given up. Yes, Jonas. I will find a little part-time job up here for September. We'll all be happier that way.

He is very pleased with himself.

13

WE carry blankets and a bottle of gin and a bucket of ice to the shade of the sweet-gum trees at the bottom of our fields, where a brook runs. We spread the blankets and Jonas makes drinks and sets down in front of Connie a bowl of dip I have made, for her to spread on crackers.

They are all there, but I am not. I am looking at us from far away, a group of pleasant cattle seen from a moving car on a hot summer's day, gathered under trees to low and munch and stay out of the heat. The children have their shoes off and are dabbling in the brook, throwing water at each other, making elaborate plans to wet us when we least expect it.

I lie on my back, wormwood in my throat, and look up at the life going on in the deep green of the trees. The sweet cries of nesting birds, the subtle walk of an inchworm divert me from the talk around me. No. It is not they that divert me. It is they that are keeping me from shouting out what is really diverting me. I diligently study the minutiae of nature to still the clamor in my head.

Bud, busting out of his Levi's, is telling us what our place is worth on today's market. I wish that he would ask for a pair of scissors to cut his pants legs off. It makes me hot just to think of him encased in denim on a day like this.

"It doesn't do us any good," Jonas is saying. "We don't plan to sell it."

No, we don't plan to, Bud. We plan to stay here for a long, long time.

They lean against the tree trunks and drink and watch the children in the brook and talk desultorily in the heat about the going price for unimproved farm land, rising taxes, the housing development in the late pasture down the road, the population explosion in our green little world. They speak of how we are being encroached upon in many ways and from many different directions. "The population of this country is supposed to double in a decade," says Bud gloomily. "Christ, we're being surrounded by a mass of fornicating humanity. Why don't they *do* something about it?"

A pair of sparrows darts busily in and out of the tree. Either they are late arrivals this year, or their first nest has been disturbed. Or maybe they have been divorced and are starting out again with new partners. Do birds marry and divorce? They call out to each other in busy domesticity as they pass in flight. "Here's a nice bit of red yarn from the boy's mitten."

"Look here, some of that good cotton batting from around the windows in the barn."

"I'm going up by the house to find some of those combings that were so soft last year."

"Don't use those barberry twigs; they prick me so."

"How about some dried timothy? You like that, don't you?"

"Why don't *you* do something about it?"

"Like what?"

"Get a vasectomy."

"Are you kidding." He har har hars. "Nobody's messin' with *my* doodles. Right, Jonas?"

"Right," says Jonas.

"It won't affect your performance, lover," says Connie, draining her glass and handing it to Jonas.

Jonas makes more drinks. He looks at me from far away. And then comes over and sits next to me and strokes the back of my neck. "I think there ought to be a sterilizing pill that you take after you've had two."

"*You* take?"

"No. *You* take."

"I think there ought to be one that you take," she says.

"Har, har, har. How'd you like to shoot blanks every night, Jonas?"

"Oh, shut up, you great vulgar beast," she says. "He doesn't do it every night and neither do you."

"Har har har." He grabs her leg and tries to bite it. They roll around on the ground and then she extricates herself and sits up, looking ruffled and annoyed. He subsides, but I can see him licking his mental chops at the thought of getting at her later. He makes another gin and tonic for himself. "Good Christ," says Jonas. "I'm glad there's not a blight on the juniper bushes."

Har har har.

The day is getting only more beautiful as it wears on, making my desolation only more difficult to bear. The smells of cut grass and earth, the heady wine of a strawberry bush up by the house, the mock orange or perhaps honeysuckle wafting from the tangled woods on the other side of the brook take me ever farther into my other world. I

94

try to imagine what he is doing this Sunday afternoon in the South, while hearing through the net of my thoughts the three around me discuss the political and aesthetic aspects of feminine hygiene deodorants. Connie regards them as another attempt by the male chauvinist advertising pigs to make women feel unworthy and unclean. "I'd like to see them come up with one for men," she says. "That would represent a quantum leap forward for Western civilization."

Har har har.

"You laugh. You could use one yourself."

"Oh, Bruce, thweetie," says Bud, slapping the air with a limp hand. "How shall I put it on, with a powder puff?"

They all laugh. I laugh a little too. It is all so absurd. Why did I have to give him up. He was so good for me. Capricorn loves Unicorn. A Unicorn is a symbol of purity.

She and I go back to the house to get the food ready, and Bud follows us, in his cowboy boots kicking daisies. To pee, he says, but I think he is hoping to back Connie up against a wall someplace in my house. Jonas stays by the brook to watch the children and to get the charcoal fire started.

We move around the kitchen doing our work. She knows where everything is and slices cheese and onions and tomatoes while I make hamburger patties. Bud urinates at length and loudly in the powder room next door. He hangs around hopefully in the kitchen for a while and then, discouraged by our busyness, lurches back to the blankets. I am sorry to see him go. I do not want to be alone with Connie.

She darts to the back door to make sure he has left. "I've just got to tell you about George," she hisses. "I've just got to."

"I really don't want to hear it, Connie."

"You'll like him. Won't you come over some morning to meet him?"

"Morning? Doesn't he work?"

"He teaches at the Community College."

"In the afternoon?"

"At night. He's a writer."

"He writes in the afternoon?"

"Oh, don't be a poop. I don't know when he writes," she says crossly. "He's writing all the time, in his mind."

For a mind-reading public. I cover my patties with Saran Wrap and start to mix the potato salad.

"I spend hours every day thinking up witty remarks for him to use in one of his novels," she says dreamily. She stands at the little mirror hanging on my cork board and examines her face, trying to see herself as he sees her.

I see myself in her. "What's the point of it all? Now you're his slave as well as Bud's."

"What do you mean by that?" She doesn't turn but eyes me through the mirror.

"You're supposed to be so liberated. You spend half your life waiting on Bud and now the other half trying to get a bit part in some idiot's nonexistent novel. Why don't you live your own life?"

"Oh, don't give me that shit," she says coldly, turning to face me. "You and Jonas with your neat little marriage all tidy and perfect. You think you've got everything, but do you ever really talk to each other? Have you ever really talked to anybody? Why don't you come down off your pedestal some day and find out what it's like to make contact. It might do you some good."

People do run to clichés in the flush of anger. I contemplate dropping the bowl of potato salad on the floor and walking out. But that would be the biggest cliché of all. So I just say, "Why don't we load the wagon?" And I think, *Contact. You're telling me about contact?* Ian's face is plastered on my own. He is my contact.

"I'm sorry." She looks stricken at what she has done.

I shrug. "It's nothing." Yes, it's nothing. You've told me what you think, and you're probably quite right. Yes, Connie. Everything you said is true. I have been a lover of tidy marriages.

We load the boys' red wagon so politely and helpfully that it takes twice as long as necessary. We take awkward turns pulling it down through the field to the others.

14

JUNE lengthens out its rare days, lighting them with a sunny beauty that flecks the lawn with gold and dapples even me as I wait for Ian in my little walled garden in the mornings.

I sit on the green bench among my tarragon and peace roses, my pear blossoms, my basil, my oregano and parsley, their scents rising around me with the sun, and listen to the buzzing of the honey bees, my eyelids hot and heavy with sun. Yes, I am waiting for Ian. He said if I would let him come he would put no pressure on me. How will it be, then? Alone on my acres, alone in the vast world of love and betrayal I have entered all by myself—no one knows where I am, really am—I think my thoughts of him and of how it will be when he comes.

In the afternoons of these waiting days, I drive the boys over back roads to a blue lake where they splash and dog-paddle in the water while I let my body darken and my hair lighten in the sun. I wave to Connie on a distant blanket. Cordially correct we are, we waiting women. One day we meet in the bath house, and she admires my tan whose outlines my new Pucci underwear is cut to match. "I like your undies too," she says. "Aren't you getting gay in your old age?" She has been wearing these flimsy nothings for years, but I have just begun.

I go again and again to the rooms over the barn, airing them daily, taking care to close the windows before Jonas comes home from work. What was originally the window that the hay was pitched out of when a farmer lived in this place is now a sliding thermal pane for a little apartment that Bud tells us we could get three hundred dollars a month for.

There is one large room with a kitchenette. The floor is covered with a rug of woven rattan, scratchy to my bare feet as I walk around looking at everything, wondering how it will seem to him. There is a studio couch with bolsters along one wall, covered in a rough white and beige cloth woven in Greece, a dark brown butterfly chair, mine from long ago, a bookcase filled with paperbacks we have read and old textbooks we do not want in the house, a maple coffee table, various wrought iron lamps, and a magazine rack with a missing spindle.

The windows are equipped with bamboo screens that roll up and down. I have tested them to make sure they work. Under the cover of the studio couch are clean sheets and on the shelf in the old oak wardrobe is a pillow, its case hand-ironed by me.

Have I gone mad. From where I lie on the couch I can look out over the fields to the willow trees down by the brook. Am I really going through with this. Tell me you'll be there when I come, I hear him say. I won't hurt you or take anything away from you. I only want to know you, to know that the woman I was born for is alive and well. Please let me come.

He is coming, though I am afraid of what it is going to mean to my tidy marriage, to the way I live. It makes me sick, the conflict and the anxiety on the one hand, and the rage to see him on the other.

He calls from a gas station to make sure I am alone and arrives five minutes later while a great green frog with palpitating throat is still struggling to break out of my chest. I hear the screen door bang behind me, and I hear my sandals slap over the flagstones. That is how I know I am going to him.

He is unwinding his body out of the car, whose windshield I notice is covered with the bodies of moths. He has driven all night to get here. I never knew Pittsburgh was so far away.

The gravel stops crunching. That is how I know I have put up my cheek to be kissed. You live in a pretty place, I think I hear him say. I don't remember what I say.

I am diffident. I look at him for a long time to see who it is who has come into my life this year and changed things. And then I take him on a tour of the house, but only the outside of it. I do not want to take him in.

When there is no more to see, I point out the willows and the brook, but he taps his chest and says, let's just sit for a minute. Mine feels constricted too. I can hardly breathe.

We sit on the green wooden bench in the walled garden, and I tell him something about walled gardens, and how I saw one in Savannah, and how I laid the bricks for this one, and espaliered the rose bushes and the pear trees and planted the herbs, and how I clip the grass myself every week with a hand clipper. He looks at my hands, and I am afraid he is going to be banal and pick one up to look for calluses, but instead he says, walled gardens. Isn't there a famous walled garden in Henry James?

I can't think of one. "Are you sure?"

"No. Not sure. I've just read a biography of him, by the way—his feminine mystique and all that."

"Oh! Do you like him?"

"I like all the Victorians," he says, a bit piously.

"Ian! Me too!" His piety is *dear*. He wants to impress me with his literariness. "Have you read the new biography of Strachey, then?"

"Yes! They were all queer."

"Yes. Even Keynes."

"Keynes. Poor Keynes. And Forster, too."

"And T. E. Lawrence. Famous for it. Do you like *him?*"

"*Love* him!" We've got a hero in common, and we talk excitedly about Lawrence and his sadomasochism, his dark poetry, even about Peter O'Toole dancing in the desert. Now that we have *him*, we know what wavelength we're on, and we take off from there into the nineteenth century. We like D. H. Lawrence, too, and Hardy, and suddenly he says, "I know where it was, the walled garden. Isn't there one at Rossetti's house in Chelsea, right after the scene in Boston when Fowles imitates James?"

"Yes! I think there is one, a sort of one, with blue wisteria, wasn't it?" Beautiful! An associative mind. And more than that, he's read Fowles! Dear Fowles, mingling old and new so trickily. I love you, Ian!

My reserve melts. I take the plunge. "You must be hungry," I say. "Why don't you take your suitcase up to the barn?"

"I've left it at a motel outside of Stamford," he says. I am so happy I could dance. "Thank you," I say. "Thank you. Thank you. Ian. I was so afraid of it." His staying *here*.

In the house we drink ale in the kitchen while I grill cheese sandwiches with sauerkraut on them. He sits at the island counter and watches me move about in the wisteria-blue dress I have bought for him. It is cut in deeply to the neck, leaving bare the shoulders I have tanned for him. He reaches out to touch me once as I move past him, and I stop and stand still for a second like a cat that wants to be stroked. We eat, our eyes glancing on and off each other. A little light goes on in my head when they meet, like the stereo beacon that lights up on our tuner when the dial pointer coincides with the right frequency on the scale. I think I would like to go on like this forever, to eat and drink and love right into the grave with him.

After lunch I show him the rest of the downstairs. He says he knew the living room would look like it should be photographed for the *New York Sunday Times* magazine.

I sit on the white linen couch from Design Research and listen while he tries our piano. I remember having heard him play in Miami at the meeting last year, but I never knew he had played jazz piano in a nightclub for three years. Ian, you surprise me so.

He eats grapes while he plays, never seeming to miss a note, even when, once, he throws a grape up in the air and catches it in his mouth. When he finishes playing, he does his grape act again and again, never missing, until I ache from laughing at the absurdity of it.

Next he wants to see my kitchen cupboards. He pulls out canned soup and shows me monosodium glutamate on the label. He pulls out three different boxes of dried cereal and shows me BHT and BHA added to packaging material to preserve freshness. And lysine hydrochloride. *That* sounds yummy, he says. He pulls out a package of starch, salt, vegetable shortening, cheddar cheese, artificial flavorings and colorings, wheat gluten, luctose, monosodium glutamate, potassium and calcium phosphates, sodium caseinate, polysorbate 60, soy protein, corn syrup, sodium silico aluminate, glycerol monostearate, sodium sulfate, BHA, and citric acid accompanied by dehydrated potatoes, onions, and celery: scalloped potatoes. "You should know what happened to the Plodding family," he says. "They ate a totally synthetic Thanksgiving dinner last year to save cooking time, and they all died the next day."

"But we have to eat something."

"Well, don't eat this crap." He adds a box of chocolate dessert mix to the pile he is building up on the counter. (Sugar, hydrogenated coconut and soybean oils, corn syrup solids, whey solids, cocoa processed with alkali, modified tapioca starch, gelatin propylene glycol monostearate, sodium caseinate, acetylated monoglycerides, sodium silico aluminate, artificial color, hydroxylated lecithin, salt, cellulose gum, malt extract, sodium stearoyl-2-lactylate, artificial flavor, BHA, and citric acid.) "How do you know what it's doing to your insides? You've been eating some of this junk for thirty years already. Look at this. Pickles!"

"So what's wrong with pickles?"

"Polysorbate eighty. Who the hell knows what that is?"

I really never thought that much about it. He is so *good*, so *virtuous*. He makes me feel so *stupid*, so nutritionally *unclean*.

"Bouillon cubes. Jesus, woman. You could kill your whole gang with some of this stuff in here. You haven't been doing your homework." He adds the bouillon cubes (hydrolized vegetable protein, salt, chicken broth, sugar, chicken fat, malto-dextrin, flavorings, spices, parsley, disodium inosinate, disodium guanylate) and a jar of mayonnaise (ingredients proprietary information of the manufacturer) to the pile and tells me to make my own.

"Don't throw out the cereal, please, Ian. We won't have anything for breakfast."

"What's wrong with the Granola I sent you?"

"They're sick of it. And Jonas won't eat it."

"Eat eggs, then, and Thomas's whole wheat. No calcium propionate added to retard spoilage. Or make oatmeal. No carcinogens added to the packing material."

"I'll try harder."

"Because?"

"Because you want me to." Because I love you. He touches me with his eyes.

I watch as he dumps twenty dollars' worth of dry goods into the trash can outside the back door. "Before I leave, we should go to the supermarket together," he says. "So I can get you off on the right foot."

"Just give me a list." Hello, young lovers, Connie trills, at the checkout counter in my head.

We walk down through the field of ripening grass, heat rising around us from the earth and with it the smells of a summer afternoon. What did someone say? The two most beautiful words in the English language? Henry James said it.

The brook is very low. I am disappointed that it is not performing better for you. We take off our sandals, and step into the water. I see you see my toes get wet. We walk on rocks barely wet down the stream bed, and sit on the grassy bank and stare into the water. A locust clicks out the time and the temperature, and bees drone in the honey-suckle, lazy, louder than the tiny silver airplane high above us. A dog barks far away. Everything seems far away. My peonies tremble beneath the sun, and across the brook raspberries seem to swell and ripen on the canes. Summer afternoon. A time for children. But we are not children, and there is something unsaid and undone that hangs in the air. I point out the sweet-gum trees with their star-shaped leaves, but you say, Lily, let's lie down somewhere. I can't talk with my head up any more.

So we go up to the barn through the grass in a quiet way, our sandals in hand, and lie down on our backs on the studio couch, looking up at the high-pitched whitewashed ceiling. A little breeze blows through the room from south to north, but it is still very very hot. I turn my face to look at you, to let you kiss me if you want to, but you only want to return my gaze. You raise yourself on your elbow and touch my face with the tips of your fingers; like a blind man reading you read me. I lie perfectly still, a cat again.

After a while I turn over so I can be on my elbow too, and we talk softly, our faces almost touching, saying what it is we like about each other, what it is that makes us know that this is meant to be. He tucks a strand of hair behind my ear and tells me things. "Do you believe me?"

Yes.

"One night I had a dream that we were together, and when I woke I could hear Becky snoring next to me."

Did you cry? Because your eyes are getting wet now. I kiss them. "We missed each other, somehow," you say.

"Yes." We missed each other somehow.

We lie on our sides and kiss slowly and quietly with our eyes open. And after a while you lean over me and undo my blue dress down the back. I offer neither help nor resistance. You sweep my back and find it clear of straps and kiss my shoulder. For an hour you caress me while our faces whisper and touch and my fears diminish. You stop always where my tan stops, though the dress does not open far enough for you even to see where that is.

I am not aggressive, and I am puzzled to find that you are not either. You have only undone my dress. I wonder how you can stand not to do any more.

And then I realize what you are doing. You are making me do it. Like in Savannah, at the bar.

I lie still again for a very long time while you stroke the small of my back where I decline and flare again.

"How can you stand this?" I hear my own pulse drumming in my head.

You only look at me, but your eyes say something.

"You're making me do it, then?"

"Yes."

"So I'll be sure?"

"Yes."

"It's hard for me."

"I know."

"Help me, then." We sit up.

You slide the blue dress off my shoulders and look at me. I shrink. I am afraid you will not like me but you bend to kiss me.

When we are both undressed we lie without touching, just to look. I have seen only Jonas. I touch you. You are so small and sweet and rosy, Ian! But there is something else. I don't know what. And then I think. "You're not circumcised?"

"No."

"Oh."

You see my chagrin—at what? at not having known what it is I am looking at?—and hug me.

"I love you," I whisper. It is so hard for me to say.

What follows I can't think of as adultery. It is just loving. I feel only utter happiness after it. I feel that I would give up everything to have you like this forever.

15

WHAT'S for dinner?" He throws his briefcase in the back seat and gets in next to me. I have had to meet the 7:07 because I put his car in for a tune-up this week so he can't take an early train home, as he sometimes does to surprise me when the boys are away, and drive up while Ian is with me. He kisses my cheek, and I smell the sweat on him and the city. I have not had time even to wash, and I reek also. Adultery is not nice.

"Cold chicken. Something light."

"Good." We wait at a light and I look at him and let him see my face. What does he see there? Nothing. It must be there, if he only had the eyes. The light changes, and he turns away. We drive on like two store dummies, looking straight ahead, our lips moving.

"The air conditioning broke down on the train. It was murder. And I had to fire Anderson today. He was not overjoyed."

"Take a nice shower. I'll make you a gin and tonic."

"Lily. You're the only one I can count on. Do you know that?" I keep on looking straight ahead. He turns to me to caress my bare brown leg, a husband's possessive gesture.

While he is in the shower, I bathe Ian off me quickly in the boys' bathroom and when he comes clean and hearty and in possession of himself again into the bedroom, I am lying there for him to have.

I don't know what I have done or why, or what I am going to do, or what there is in me that makes me false twice in one day. But I am strangely calm and feel no guilt at all, and after dinner, when we walk down through the fields to the brook in the moonlight and talk about how we should try to convince the neighbors downstream to let us dam the brook for swimming, I think, Nothing has changed. It's as if it never happened. I wonder if this is because he is not in tune with me, or simply because I have understood so well how to deceive him into thinking I am in tune with him.

But later, in bed, I lie awake for a while and wonder if tomorrow, when I look in the mirror, I will see a coarsening and creasing, an inner vileness showing through. There must be some price to pay for what I have done.

Ian brings a box of raspberries in the morning and we eat them with cream in the sunny kitchen and later we go up to the barn to make love. When it is over, I think how different it is from what I am used to: Jonas's businesslike and soundless efficiency when he bends to the same task. I am amazed, in fact, at all the differences there are. It had not occurred to me that the same act could go through such a drastic permutation when the actor changed. There is even something comical about it, his being so small and yet so quick and powerful for me, and I laugh inside to myself. He feels the silent cadenza of mirth in my chest and raises his head to look at me. Hello. Hello.

We take a shower, lathering each other tenderly. I stand back to admire him as the clean water rinses away the suds on his nice self. I love him.

He makes me run back to the house with only a towel around me for a scissors and hair dryer, and he cuts my hair, which he says is too long for my face.

I stand still and naked on a towel spread on the floor to catch the clippings, and he moves naked around me, a towel around his waist.

I didn't know he had worked as a hairdresser. A Renaissance man I have.

I study him as he works. His body is healthy and fine. I clasp him to me and kiss the hollows under his collarbone. His gray eyes kiss me back. They love me.

When he has finished my hair, he blows it dry with my hand dryer. I think I look rather like a raspberry. My new hairdo muffins around my face in a soft puff, like the small round drupelets we have eaten. He tells me its name; it is called the surfer cut. I look young and rosy and innocent.

I am innocent. I have no idea of what the consequences will be of what I am doing. I only know he is for me, and I am going to have him.

We are familiar with each other today and make free. It is our last day together, but we explore each other with a luxurious slowness, as if we have all the time in the world. It is only in the afternoon when the shadows lengthen toward us from across the lawn that we realize it is almost over. We grow somber and still and lie together. I kiss his eyes and his battered nose and his perfect mouth and try to tell him what he is to me. Now there is a hopelessness in the air, a sense of having missed the boat. It is a time for promises, but what can we promise.

"Stay here tonight," I beg him. "I'll come out when Jonas goes to sleep."

He is torn. I see it in his eyes. "No, I can't."

"Please. He won't know."

"I can't."

"I'll meet you then."

"Where?"

"At the end of the driveway at a certain time."

He thinks. "No," he says finally. "We've taken enough chances. We'll be caught. Anyway, I checked out of the motel this morning. I have to start back."

"Why? Why tonight?"

"Because Becky thinks I flew to New York, so I have to be in Pittsburgh in the morning."

His reasonableness infuriates me. What Becky thinks has nothing to do with us. "I don't care! Ian. I love you. I don't want you to go."

He holds me. "You care. And it matters how we do this. If we're going to keep on."

"Are we then?"

"Aren't we?"

"But for how long can we?" Forever? Like this?

"For as long as you want."

"As *I* want?"

"I'll never stop."

I am discomfited again. It is his passivity that bothers me. He leaves everything to me. And his acting as if he is some sort of object that I can keep or discard as it pleases me: I do not like that. How can I value him if he doesn't value himself?

But he will be gone in a few hours, and I can think those hard things when I am alone.

And then we hear the car grinding up the gravel driveway. I know without looking that they have brought the boys back a day early. That was why the phone in the house was ringing this morning.

We are prepared for it, in some ways. We dress in rapid expert movements, smooth the bed, put the pillow in the wardrobe. The room looks as it did before we came to it. Except that we cannot close the windows without being seen.

The boys, shouting "Mom," are running around the house, looking for me, and my mother, seen from above, looks damp and irked. She peers around the yard for me, and then walks into the house, followed by my father. The screen door slams shut, and I hear them yoo-hoo for me in the house. "Good-bye," he says.

"Good-bye."

"I'll be back."

"I don't know yet what I'm going to do."

"Don't do anything drastic." What does that mean?

He looks at me, waiting for me to go.

"I'm not sorry for anything," I say. "I just don't know whether I'll be able to go on with two lives."

"I know."

"We're leaving on Saturday."

"Will you write?"

"If I can. Yes."

"I'll be back when you want me."

I want you now. Don't go.

"Run now," he says.

"Yes." Ian.

"Good-bye. I love you."

"Good-bye." Ian. Ian. I kiss him quickly on the mouth. A brief taste of him is all I have as I run down the stairs and into the field of sun and shadows where my sons are searching for me.

"*There* you are. Where have you been all day?" My mother, querulous from the heat.

"Swimming this morning. Why did you come back to-day?"

"Swimming. And there we were in the hottest place in Connecticut."

New Haven must be hotter than Goshen. "I'm sorry."

"Where were you just now? The boys are out looking for you."

"Down by the brook."

"I called you all morning to tell you we were bringing them back. Peter cried for you the whole time. I couldn't take it."

"I'm sorry."

"Whose car is that outside with the Georgia license plates?"

"A handyman."

"What are you having done?"

"I was showing him the brook to see what he thought about damming it for swimming."

"Not safe. The boys'll be drowning in it. Besides the Gillies won't let you. There he goes now." She stands on tiptoe to get a look at him through the kitchen window. "Probably left a wife and six kids on welfare down South," she says grimly.

"Do you mind if I lie down for a few minutes?"

"Better find those boys first," she says. "I can't keep up with them. And I don't suppose you have anything in for supper. Not expecting us."

"I'll make a tuna salad. Just let me go upstairs for a minute."

I flee to my room and shut the door and lie so still on my white plissé bedspread that I fancy I can hear him still breathing and whispering next to me. But he is out on the highway by now, heading home.

The boys ferret me out; they could find a millet seed in a wind tunnel. They climb on top of me, paper me with

112

kisses, beg me to go outside to play with them. I press them to me, my little Indians, smelling their baby skin and hair. I wonder how they would remember me if I should go, if Peter would remember me at all, what Jonas would have to say about me then. "Darlings, leave me be tonight. I have such a headache from the sun. Will you ask Granny to make you all a tuna salad and leave some for Daddy?" They smooth my forehead, their faces puckering anxiously at my bad news, and troop stoically away. I get up to pull down the shades and lie down again in the darkened room to relive what we have done together. Detail by detail, I reconstruct the two days, engraving it on my memory so that if I am never so happy again I will never forget what I have had.

When Jonas comes home, I get up to stand at the window to listen to what my mother has to say. She tells him that I didn't answer the phone all morning, that a handyman from Georgia was here when they arrived, and that I have another one of my headaches. She senses a connection among these random facts. Yankee, go home, I think.

I lie down again and think of her word for women like me: *Bum.* It isn't a nice word, especially the way she says it. She said *Gypsy* the same way when I had my ears pierced a few weeks ago.

He comes at dusk, big cat padding down the hall. He lies next to me in the dark and strokes my back. I feel only dullness and pain. He cannot see my face, and for that I am grateful. Perhaps he could see tonight that I am not the woman he thought I was. What is life except to be good to those who love you. Oh, Jonas, I have been so bad to you.

"You had one of these headaches not long ago."

"Yes." He doesn't remember where or when.

"Do you think it's anything serious? Should you see a doctor?"

"No."

"Is it about working?"

"No. Nothing like that."

"What, then?"

"Nothing."

I tell him only that he must arrange to send the boys away in the morning so I can be alone for a day to unknot my migraine, so I can calm and collect my senses, strung out now like lights on a cliff in a windstorm. Buffeted by the gale within, they flicker and sway so that I am not sure if they will last the night. I rather expect they will leave me to shriek in the storm for what I have missed in life: the oneness of soul I think we have found, only too late to be of any good to us, in each other.

I stand in the tall window in the upstairs hall in the morning and watch with a certain coldness as they drive away with Jonas to spend the day at Jo-Anne's house. I wonder if I will watch them drive away for good with him someday, for I know there is one argument he will never let me win.

What do I have of yours? I root in the trash for the empty raspberry box, wood-grain bleeding. And set it on the kitchen table beside half a bag of stale Granola, a postcard signed Mickey Mouse from Disneyland, and a picture of you at an F & F training meeting taken four years ago when your hair was short. (I hardly recognized you at first when I found the picture in Jonas's files.) That is all I have of you that I can touch.

I go back to the barn and get my scissors and hair dryer and find that we have left the fan on. I lie on the couch and go over it all in my mind again and again, feeling your presence as if you were here.

And when Jo-Anne arrives with the boys we have this
conversation:
"You're looking well, Jo-Anne."
(Blushing.) "I'm having . . . No. I shouldn't tell you."
(Bleakly.) "An affair."
"No. I'm having . . . electrolysis."
"Oh. Does it hurt?"
"No."
An affair hurts.

16

MY faculties are disarranged. I pack for vacation in such a haphazard way that I know, even as I do it, that I am doing it all wrong. Packing things we will not possibly need, umbrellas, a case of catfood when we are boarding the cat, and my pinking shears, of all things, and forgetting the citronella lamps for the porch and the clam knife and the big enamel pot for boiling the lobsters. And on Saturday, we drive off in the morning leaving the boys' bathing suits on the line and the air conditioners on in the bedrooms. We remember when we have driven an hour. Jonas is annoyed with me. I listen to his bluster without caring. I don't even want to go this year.

Jo-Anne is having . . . electrolysis. And when she is finished with it, then she is going to have an affair. Every wife deserves *one*, she says. And what's the point of waiting till you're too old to look good?

How do other women do this thing so easily? It is driving me crazy, the morality of it.

Jo-Anne has a thing about growths, hirsute or otherwise. She goes once a year to a dermatologist for a complete physical, the way other women go to their gynecologist for an annual Pap test. She lies unclothed on a table while he examines her with a magnifying glass—every mole and freckle and minor excrescence passes under his scrutiny. She is always having something or other removed. This year it is unsightly hair.

Connie refers to her as B. O. Bradshaw behind her back, because she doesn't use a deodorant. Jo-Anne believes they are carcinogenic.

I have little growths too. Little evil ones on the inside of my mind. But nobody knows they are there. I can feel them growing and writhing around in my head, extending little tentacles, little fine roots, into the hollow space behind my forehead. They are making me dizzy.

Jonas likes my new haircut. He reaches out to stroke it at a stop light. "So soft," he says. "It suits you."

I lie about the place in town where I had it done.

I give the lie, but the lie gives me vague adumbrations of treacheries played out against me. I feel uneasy. Nothing is nice any more. Maybe I am going to have a nervous breakdown.

If only he had stayed to meet me once more. Taken another chance for me.

Connie, Jo-Anne, Claudine, I think as we drive along, do you have lovers because like me you need a man to make you feel like somebody? Oh, darlings, how sad for us if that's the way it is. Why can't we feel like somebodies on our own?

We are going the back way, driving to New London so we can take the ferry to Orient Point and go the Shelter Island-Sag Harbor way on to the Hamptons. We do this to avoid having to see what has become of the landscape the other way in the last years. But it is almost as bad this way.

"Pe-yew," the boys shout, diving under their car quilties. "What's that stink?" We hastily roll up all the windows in the car. Pfizer Chemicals are fouling the New London air. Jonas has missed the exit and now has to backtrack to the ferry slip. I was supposed to be watching for it. We are not off to a very good start this year.

I dutifully begin to collect the debris from the trip. Several empty pint containers of milk, eggshells, orange peels, browning apple cores, and a box that a few hours ago contained forty-eight Fig Newtons. None of it was consumed by me. I have no appetite today. I am merely the garbage collector for this outfit. But I have forgotten a plastic bag to put it all in, so I stuff it into the milk containers and stuff them into my beach bag. "Good girl," says Jonas. The prospect of sea air is improving his mood already.

17

J ONAS is running backwards down the beach, limbs at
unfamiliar angles. A flock of children, sons and nieces,
runs with him, wishing skyward the diving leaping kite he
is winding out, a chrome yellow box dancing against the
deep blue curtain of sky. Beyond, the sky dives too, to meet
the dancing blue sea at the hinge of the horizon.

All is in such absolutes today. Absolute colors, absolute
directions, absolute forms, absolute values. This is good,
our being here together: our marriage, our family. Everything that diminishes it is bad. My love for Ian is bad.

Is my love for Ian bad? That question has been haunting
my head for two weeks. If one sees things in absolutes as
Jonas does, then the answer must be yes. But my imagina-
tion feeds on gradients that his does not admit. One loves
Jonas, or one does not. One is married to him, or one is
not. Yet, I love him, and I love Ian too, and I am married
to Ian in a way I have never been married to Jonas, as a
kite is married to the sky—briefly, wondrously, recklessly.
Remember the first fine careless rapture? Remember lives
of quiet desperation? These two phrases chase each other

in and out of my head till I think I will go crazy.

And as there are fewer ticks on Jonas's continuum of possibilities, so is there a difference too in the range we know. He has a richer middle ground, perhaps, finding deeper satisfaction in what we have. But then he does not imagine what we don't have. Things are seldom what they seem, Jonas. We have in this hand the reality that is you, and in this hand the mirror that is me, reflecting the appearance of your reality, which is to say a reality so removed from reality that who is to say what is what. What does it all mean? Whom shall I mirror? Whom shall I marry? Are these even the right questions?

The kite is up now. He will soon be anchoring it in the sand for its day on high, and coming back to me. Today is his last day here. He will want to lie on the army blanket next to me and probe my feelings about staying alone with the boys until next weekend, when he will come out again. "Will you be all right alone?" he will ask. "Do you have enough to read?" Yes, Jonas. Yes, dear. He will want to review our two weeks together, to assure me that the weather will stay fine. The weather has been the best we have had in eight years here, and I hope it will hold, because the gloom of gray clouds lowering would finish me. I am just hanging in there with the help of the sun.

I have written to Ian many times since he left seventeen days ago, but I have mailed none of the letters, not for lack of opportunity. At first, I did not want my love thoughts to grow cold in a post-office box in Savannah while he mingled in Pittsburgh with in-laws, and then there is something else, too, something subtle and complex that has come over me. I do not yet understand what it is, but I am thinking about it all the time, trying to figure it out.

It has something to do with being here and with our

feelings, Jonas's and mine, that we will not be coming here again, that this place is not good for us any more. Ian has something to do with the reasons for that, but just what is not so obvious as it might seem. Don't do anything drastic, he said, and I think he meant, don't tell your husband what you've done.

This has been "our" place for eight years. Teddy was conceived here, and Peter was unexpectedly born here one early August morning, in the Southampton hospital, popping out of my aching thighs in the entrance foyer, the way a ripe tomato dropped in boiling water will pop out of its skin. I nursed them here, trained them here, helped them take their first steps here. They have had their first fishing poles here, first caught frogs here, in the marshy grass by the bay, and as they have grown, we have rejoiced here to think of the idyllic summers we are giving them, a summer "place" we have meant them to be able to recall in later life as an anchor in a world that has devalued anchors.

But the place has changed. It has caught on with people who look strange to us, and unappetizing. There are more cars now, more boutiques full of loony clothes and loony people, more bars, more weird houses sitting uncomfortably in gone potato fields. We have tried to compensate, have sought ever more un-frisbeed sands to lie upon, ever more deserted waters to swim in, but there are no more to discover. The whole shoreline is peopled.

We changed our pattern of restaurant-going a couple of years ago, staying in on weekends and dining out, Jonas and I, only midweek, when the illusion of quiet old times could be maintained. But this year we haven't even bothered with that. We gave up shellfish last year, and this year we have passed up the rest, despite the newspaper clippings taped in the fishmonger's window assuring that the dangers

of mercury poisoning are greatly exaggerated. Besides, the
fishmonger himself has changed. He has grown some ex-
traordinary sideburns and has expanded into the shop next
door and now caters clambakes and advertises a bagel and
lox special on Sunday mornings and wears a vinyl apron
that says on it, *Blow in my ear and I'll follow you anywhere.* We avoid him.

We have kept up with a few returning families, sharing
with them an aversion to what is going on. We have stalled,
demurred, kept to ourselves, tried not to expose our children to the new culture around us, as if it were something
lethal that would harm them. We have bought from the
farms as much as possible to avoid having to connect with
the new people in the supermarkets, shopping for their
canned clam bisque and frozen fried scallops, buying their
pre-shredded salad greens.

We have stayed together, we families, building a little
bulwark against the change swirling around us, but the
change is as impossible to avoid as the changes we find in
the shoreline each returning June. Clambakes are catered
now, we cannot or will not eat the local fish, and some of
the old families have not come back this year. Jonas says
we must go farther away to find what we want.

Yesterday, we were planning to take the boys and their
cousins to the duck farm, but in Friday's paper we read that
the ducks were all slaughtered, their necks wrung by van-
dals in the night. I have not slept since, for two nights. I
lie awake and think of the sound the necks make when they
break, and of what a duck thinks when he senses his turn
coming.

We are glad now that we did not buy the cottage when
we had a chance to several years ago. We will have to find
a new place, Jonas says. Try to start over somewhere else

to give the boys a tie, a sense of place, a sense of good old summer days to lend perspective to the crazy times.

He is lying next to me now, back from kite-flying. Innocent. He thinks we are happily married.

He has no conception of the extremes I am trying to weather.

What have I done? What is life except to be good to those who love you? What sadness, what abiding sadness I feel, to think I have not been good.

A wave of nausea passes over me when I think of my so-easy defection. Really, it is gross to think that the first chance I got in seven years to cuckold him I took. And so, I try not to think of it. I think instead, To thine own self be true. I think, Life is to play on the whole keyboard. I think, Life *is* extremes, for those who can feel them. I think, Life is to live, to go to the mountaintop. All that sort of thing. It makes me feel better. But still the mangled ducks and the contaminated fish and the unappetizing moderns give me nausea when my own head doesn't.

Aaron and Kathy are coming toward us now. I sit up to welcome them. They come every summer for a few days. I love to have them. Family. Another anchor in the shifting sands.

This year they have come in a camper bus and sleep in it in the back yard, but tonight, when Jonas leaves, Aaron will go too, to get the Metroliner back to Baltimore in the morning, and Kathy and the girls will move into the house, she to sleep in Jonas's bed, the cousins to double up in the boys' room on cots. I am looking forward to being alone with her for a few days.

They have been to the old Dutch cemetery this morning to copy down epitaphs. But they have returned disturbed. Some of the best headstones have been knocked over, and what Aaron calls loaded rubbers were draped over some of the other ones.

We open the wicker lunch basket they have brought and give the cousins their sandwiches and grapes. The four of them run off to their private blanket under the dunes, and we loll on our own and eat salami and cherry tomatoes and feta cheese and drink red wine. I feel normal and natural again. She buoys me, gives me the impression that all is not lost.

She is the best girl I know. Virtue incarnate, perfect wife, wise mother, she plays her role with total enthusiasm. She is blond and trim and good as gold. If she knows there's been a sexual revolution in this decade, she isn't letting on. Her swimsuit, as she calls it, which is at least as old as her marriage, is one piece and flowered, and has a built-in bra and a boxy bottom. She is small and calm and doles out seconds on grapes and tiny cans of apricot nectar with perfect justness.

She has turned Aaron and her girls into ardent Episcopalians, while I, out of a lesser conviction, I suppose, have not managed to inspire Jonas and my boys even with Unitarianism. Her children, polite little Christians, Aunt Lily me to my eyebrows, but I like my boys to have cousins, blond Episcopalian girl cousins. They are a good influence with their nice mores and manners.

I like to feel too that if anything should happen to me Kathy will take over.

If I should go away. Not that he has asked me to. And not that I have made it up in my mind that I would if he did. I don't know. I feel when I think of it all as if I am being stretched out to the snapping point. Yet the rack is of my own devising. And who is doing the stretching? Ian? Jonas? Me myself? I myself? I am no longer sure of anything.

I wonder if I am having a nervous breakdown. To give up what I have? Yet two days exist now to illuminate what it *is* that I have.

We lie motionless in the sun until a cloud comes out of nowhere and passes between it and us. Then we stir and shiver our private shivers.

I am truly afraid of being alone should the weather turn. I sit up in the grayness to judge it. The beach at both ends is still in the sun. It is gray only here in the middle where we are. After a while the cloud goes on its way, and we settle down again, except Kathy, who sits up to watch our children. They are near the water now, making a complex network of tunnels and turrets just this side of the buzzing surf.

Another family—one I have never seen here before—is assembling near us. Why do they come to the territory we have staked out? There are plenty of other places. They have teen-agers and are equipped with a radio and a portable television set with a screen-darkening panel, and a surfboard, wet suits, a polyfoam ice bucket and a lunch hamper, an inflatable mat, several beach chairs, a cosmetic case revealing mirror and lights when it is opened, which it promptly is, a big beach umbrella, and individual terry-cloth towels, which they spread out in an untidy mosaic, right under our noses.

An unwholesome foursome is setting up camp on the other side of us. They too have electronic gadgets to make them feel right at home on the beach of what they do not know was once a fishing village remote from the world.

They seem not to belong at all to the pale little boy who accompanies them and who is not encouraged to "do" anything, once they have unpacked. He stands away from them, sucking his thumb, one finger hooked over his nose stroking it, while they settle down in suspect conjunction.

Their flesh has a mushroom paleness to it, as if they have not been out in the sun before, as if they have stayed indoors all summer to play foul games with each other.

I want to move, but where? The beach is rapidly filling up with tawdry groups. I go and sit by the children and start a drip castle for them. It is slow and painless work, and I do not have to watch the crowd. But I lay my cheek on my knee as I work and listen to two young mothers, new this summer, their nipples always erect under wisps of Banlon, conferring near me. "Let's go rub up against King," says one of them, and they saunter over to the lifeguard's stand where they do indeed rub up against him.

They think their children and a hundred others are being watched by the second lifeguard, but he is mainly watching the nymphets who sport in the surf for his benefit.

Everything revolves around sex out here. Everyone is thinking it and talking it and listening to it on their transistors and doing it with their eyes. I look back at our blanket at Kathy and Aaron and Jonas. They seem unconcerned by it all, relics of a bygone age. On the other hand, the sun and the scene are stirring me against my will. I *desire* Ian. Desire him madly. I have been so disoriented by the two weeks without him after the two intense days with him that I think it is making me crazy. The high and then the low.

I think this must be the punishment I expected, the cosmic retribution exacted for stolen pleasures: the crashing down I cannot share. No one knows. I have had to crash all alone. It has left me exhausted and enervated and unstable.

Maybe all the decay I see around me is just a surface mold. Maybe everything is firm and healthy on the inside. But I don't really believe that. Teen-agers strangling ducks? They scare me, teen-agers today.

I went to church this morning, hoping to regain my equilibrium at St. John in the Woods. It is a church that I find pretty and pleasing, and there is something of real holiness about the minister. He has affected me in the past. I wished this morning to be affected again, to be led to grace.

A simple brown-shingled structure with a graceful spire and plain leaded windows, the church can seat a hundred or so, but there were only twenty of us there this morning. The altar was decorated with daisies in green glass vases, and we sang "Fairest Lord Jesus," my favorite hymn.

But the minister I knew was not in the pulpit. A guest minister with shapely auburn hair and a minuscule vocation read to us from the charter of the United Nations in an attempt to inspire us with brotherhood. I longed for him to be through with it, so we could at least get on with a hymn, but on turning to "He's the Lily of the Valley" I found an obscenity neatly lettered at the top of the page, accompanied by an informative illustration showing us exactly how He would have. Jesus? I left the church at the end of the service in a daze, neglecting to shake the guest minister's hand as I passed by him at the door. I took the hymn book home with me. I intend to erase the slander and return the book next week.

"What are you and Aaron doing to protect your girls from modern life?" I ask Kathy when we are finally alone in the evening, reading in the little flowered living room.

She looks at me strangely, "What do you mean?"

"Well, like the cemetery this morning. People who will do things like that. What are you doing about it?" I demand.

"It's an isolated case," she says. "You can't protect them from everything."

"I'm very depressed," I tell her, and my voice comes out

in a wavering high pitch. "I feel everything is rotten right through."

She stares at me, the table lamp at her side casting strange shadows on her face. "It's not normal to be depressed about something so big and vague," she says. I can only make a gesture with my hands to tell her it is so. Too hard to talk. I need her help to get me through.

"Depression comes from anger you haven't expressed," she says. "Or guilt."

"I'm not." Not what?

She goes out to the kitchen to make us some more tea. We have already had two cups. I cry noiselessly and hopelessly in the uncomfortable rattan chair. "You never find everything you want in one man," she says, setting the mug down on the coffee table in front of me. "If you care, you have to make do. The next one won't have something Jonas has."

I know.

"I left Aaron once," she says. "We didn't tell you."

A dizziness, a fluttering in a hollow spot just behind my forehead. Not Kathy. I try not to listen to the story of her lover and their trysts in the new motel on the outskirts of town. He is so romantic, keeping next to his heart always the key to a locker they rent where they keep their nightclothes and special underwear and other essentials. She tells me proudly that she has a separate diaphragm just for him.

But I don't tell her anything, except that it is just such revelations as hers that are depressing me.

"A woman has a lover," she says angrily. "What's the big revelation? Men do it." I have not seen her so aggressive before. An ugly look has taken over her face. I am afraid of her. I am afraid of all of us women.

It's that she kept it hidden, I try to tell her. She presented us with an illusion.

"And what are *you* doing? That's what's depressing you, you know. Trying to keep up some kind of illusion that you're so happy with Jonas."

"I am happy." I *was* happy.

"Happy," she sneers. "Happy. I suppose you think your lover's going to make you happy too. Well, let me tell you something."

"I never said that," I retort. But I'm not sure if I said it or not. Did I even mention "my lover"? I can't remember. Everything is swirling around in my head.

"Ha" is all she says. Her eyebrows flick derisively from above the rim of the tea mug.

There is nothing more to say, and so I say good night and go into the little bedroom where we will be sleeping together and undress quickly in the dark. While I am in the bathroom washing, she undresses in the bedroom and is in Jonas's bed, unwashed, when I return. We say good night.

It was to have been so nice, so cozy and sisterly. I lie awake for a long time listening to her breathing. I think I am going out of my mind.

But in the morning she says to me, "I'm really sorry about last night. I was drunk."

"Drunk?"

"I drink," she says.

"I didn't see you drinking."

"I was drinking out of the mug. You thought it was tea." She produces a quart bottle of bourbon from under the kitchen sink and holds it up for me to see. There is a little left at the bottom. "It was full two nights ago," she says, putting it back under the sink.

I stare at her in horror. "What are you *doing* about it?"

"Nothing. I like it." She cracks eggs into a bowl for breakfast. Six eggs, one for each of us. She washes and dries three grapefruit. "Don't just stand there. Set the table," she says pertly. She is stirring eggs, sectioning grape-fruit, toasting muffins, pouring juice, brewing coffee with the efficiency of a twenty-first-century breakfast-making machine, while I stand confounded, watching her.

I am thinking, if we're all drunks and whores, what's the point of the whole thing?

The next day, when it is time for her to leave for Balti-more, she says to me in her firm, just way, I expect you not to tell Jonas anything. She stands on tiptoe to kiss me good-bye. She looks like a tiny blond child perched high up behind the wheel of the camper bus. "When it gets out of hand, I'll do something, so don't worry," she says out of the window, the woman I was going to leave my children to.

"Good-bye, Kathy."

"Toodle-oo!" She puts the bus into gear and waves cheerily as she maneuvers it into position for going down the long driveway onto the highway. My blond nieces wave from the back windows. I stand waving till they are out of sight and then just stand for a long time, looking down the driveway bowed with firs.

I don't believe any of it, really. I think now that she must have made it all up. It couldn't be true.

"Can we have a camper bus, Mom?"

They are playing in the sandy driveway at my feet a complicated game they have invented involving seashells and sea-rounded stones.

"No," I say slowly.

"How come?"

"They cost too much, I guess."

"We'll get one when our ship comes in, Pete," says Teddy. "Won't we, Mom?"

"Maybe."

"Maybe not," says Peter. "We'll ask Daddy about it."
I am numb and dumb. I cannot talk to them. I go back
into the cottage and lie on the couch until they come in
and ask me for their dinner, hours later, it seems.

18

WHEN they are in bed, I am finally alone, for the first time since Ian. I lie on the couch in the living room and try to reconstruct our two days again in every detail, but the memories are already fading, and there are some sequences, some whispered dialogue I cannot remember at all. What were all those things he told me? I said I believed them. I did. I do. But I can't remember now what they were.

Is it all over? Is that all there is going to be? Or will there be a letter waiting for me when I get home, a letter helping me to decide how I am going to live the rest of my life?

I feel will-less, de-willed, un-willed. I cannot act until my play has a director.

But there is something . . . something disagreeably quaint about this state of mind in this day and age. I am still not my own woman. I am still Jonas's child-wife, the maiden waiting for her man. An appendage. What is it going to take to free me? I lie inert on the couch following the stagger of cracks on the ceiling, my hands folded on my breasts in an attitude of death, or of waiting. I am thinking in metaphors, the abstraction, the removal of myself from myself by one step perhaps signifying that I am coming into some new objectivity about myself. I think of myself as a colonial nation, occupied in stages by imperialistic parents, husband, children. I am struggling for self-government. I want to fly under my own flag, my motto emblazoned in red on a purple field, one woman one life to lead.

But I don't have the . . . how shall I say it?—"tits"?—to fly under my own flag. I find it painful to be vulgar let alone to be so bizarre as to actually demand a full measure of autonomy. (Connie is right; I am hopelessly repressed. I remember having had a discussion with her last year about my inability to use certain words, one in particular. She suggested that I think of it as spelled with a *ph*. I tried, but it didn't have the same . . . phlavor.)

The upshot is that I have performed my little act of rebellion, my attempt to sever the colonial ties, under false colors. Instead of running up my own flag, I have simply phlown under Ian's. I am still Jonas's woman, and what's even more depressing, I'm Ian's woman now as well.

There must be more to it than this. Some mental spring must be sprung. Or we have thrown ourselves away, so to speak, Connie and I and Claudine and Kathy. And Jo-Anne is about to. I must warn her. I must warn her that we are not going to grow up this way.

The answer lies elsewhere. Perhaps I haven't asked the right question yet. Where does one's responsibility to oneself begin and end? Where does one's responsibility to one's phamily and phellowman begin and end? (You see what I mean about *ph*'s, Connie: they reduce everything to absurdity.) I've got to get the right angle on that question. It's important. It's important not to think of it as absurd.

What perhaps is absurd is Ian and I being apart. Maybe

the question is, now that the little Ghana that I am has announced for herself, should she give up the comforts of the protectorate? We should be together, shouldn't we, Ian? You said so. And I think so. Is that the right question, then? How are Ian and I going to get rid of our encumbrances and spend the rest of our lives together? But no, there's something more to it than that. I just haven't put my finger on it yet.

I hear a car door close and seconds later a twig or a clam shell snap under the kitchen window. Panic freezes me into inaction. I think of a woman alone in a secluded seaside cottage being visited in the night by the man she fears and hates most in the world. The doorknob turns; he is framed in the way, the overhead light revealing a gleaming blade gripped at his side.

There is a quick knock on the glass pane in the front door. I spring up in terror and rush to the door, which though it is locked is easily entered. With trembling hand I push on the porch light.

It is Ian. I have hardly ever seen him in long trousers and dress shirt before. I gather him in. He has been in New York with Jonas all day, talking about Anderson's job. He has rented a car and made the long drive out here, arriving breathless in the town with no idea of where I lived. He has found me by animal instinct, sniffing me out. A blond family. Ashe. Two small boys. A Ford station wagon. Here for a month. The owner of the drugstore we use lives across the way. Ian has been to the drugstore.

He has been all around the house, too, peering through the windows to make sure I am alone. "Why haven't you written?" His face is ghastly. I kiss it and draw it to my breast, stroking his temples. I love him.

He cries, "Christ. You didn't *write!*"

"I couldn't." What was I supposed to write? "You can't believe what I've been through. And then today, a real ball-breaker." Today, in New York with Jonas, making promises, registering expectations, forecasting and reviewing, martinis for lunch, meeting Fleming himself, congratulations, calling Becky with the good news and the lie, the drive, the traffic, the uncertainty and now all the tension coming loose in a lovemaking that is as brilliant and complete as a major diamond.

We lie quietly afterward, feeling the fit of our bodies while it lasts, feeling utter peace and quiet and utter . . . happiness. That is the only word for what I feel.

He leaves at the first light of dawn, and I drift back to sleep. I feel freed and free, my future clear.

We meet again, as if by accident, on the golden windy beach at nine. The ocean stretches its blue all around us and the activity of the scene—of the ships steaming along the horizon, of the lifeguards readying their equipment for the day, of the gulls and sandpipers, and of Teddy and Peter already busily constructing a new set of tunnels and turrets—forms a counterpoint to our blissful inactivity. We turn our backs on the sun and lie calmly looking into each other's eye, feeling invisible and, I, smugly at peace.

How far we have come since Palm Beach. And yet how far have we come?

He tells me about Philadelphia and about the townhouse we can buy there on his new salary and renovate with handy urban renewal money. I think of the museums there and of how lovely it will be to live in a city again and walk to work. By the time it is all settled, a year from now, at least, the boys will be in school all day. My working will not affect them at all, Your Honor. But then, we realize, of course, that it is all a dream. Ian cannot go on working for

Jonas once Jonas's wife has announced for Ian. "That's all right," he says. "I can have my pick of jobs now that I've made it with Fleming. An offer to be Eastern Regional Manager at twenty-eight! Baldwin and Knabe will sit up and bark to get me now." He rests his chin on stacked fists and mows the dune grass with his eyes.

Teddy comes and stands next to us for a long time. I study his sturdy little legs, tanned and scabby from falls. He drops down next to me and whispers something in my ear. "Is that man going to build a dam in our brook?" His eyes are formidable as they wait for my answer. His brain is not to be taken lightly.

But I lie, of course, sitting up to tie the drawstrings on his trunks. "It's not the same man, darling," I say. I notice how his tanned stomach pops still in a baby way. "Yes, it is, Mommy," he whispers insistently. "He's just like him. See his sandals."

"Lots of men have sandals like that," I say. "Now, go play with Peter."

"Well, I know he is, Mom, because he said hi to me when he came out of the barn that day."

I shiver. "Maybe, dear. But maybe it's just two people who look alike."

He looks unconvinced and glances over at Ian again before he goes away. I see him telling Peter something. Peter looks shyly at Ian.

"You said hi to him coming out of the barn."

"Smart kid you have," says Ian. "He nearly ran right into me as I was leaving."

I am silent, thinking of lies I have told and lies I will tell. But I don't really care now. I have decided how I want things. I feel exhilarated by it, liberated almost, this hard decision made.

19

IT is Ian's wish that we meet once more before we tell
Jonas and Becky. Is there something you don't like
about me? No, he answers, on Fleming stationery. I just
want you to be perfectly sure.
He wants to be perfectly sure. But that's all right. I want
him to be, too. He has to give up his children *and* his job
for me.
It will all be shocking to Jonas. I wish there were some
way of doing it without his knowing who the man is—his
own beautiful Ian.
I fly to Savannah in an airplane upholstered in beige
and paneled in turquoise shot with long-pointed silver stars.
There are only a dozen passengers to start, though more get
on and some get off at the stops along the way. Baltimore,
Richmond, Raleigh, Charleston: an endless series of short
flights linked together with landings and takeoffs that
soon have my stomach jumping and my nerves on edge.
Or maybe it is what I am doing that gives me this sick
feeling in my stomach.
Looking down, I am surprised as always when I fly to see

mainly woodland and open pasture. Green suburbs fringe minor cities. I wonder if they are mistaken, the ecologists and the ZPG people, or if they knowingly lie. Why shouldn't they? Everybody else does.

I follow roads that wind like tape through pleasant miniature landscapes, and wish that I could look at myself from afar and miniaturize my crowded mindscapes into insignificance.

Coffee and pastries are proferred constantly by the stewardesses, and I consume too much of them, out of nervousness. I have a bulkhead seat and make frequent trips up the long aisle to the lavatory.

I am wearing sandals, and my bare toes keep curling under of their own will, despite my admonitions to them to lie straight, and a yellow linen dress, a 1970 update of the kind of dress I have always worn. At least I have not been quick to change my looks. Only the frosty mauve lips and the silver on my eyelids and the authentic-looking blush on my cheeks, seen in the mirror of the tiny lavatory, are new and different. My face, though one might think adultery would harden it, is in fact softer and prettier than before. Ian's haircut, falling into puffy muffs at my ears, softens me. Even the wrinkles gathering at the corners of my eyes and making crescents around my mouth seem to soften me, as they did not when I wore bright orange on my mouth and tucked my hair behind my ears. I am pleased with myself, most of all because I still look like myself. Tall, mild, decorous, and behind the times; still Lily, despite my plunge into the times.

Yes, jetting southward to meet my lover, a recent tubal ligation, his idea, assuring me a perfect freedom, and Vivian, an old friend in Boston, my idea, a perfect cover, I feel very much in the swim. A modern mother, my children behind me safe at Granny's, my lover ahead of me growing amorous in the airport, and my husband, like me, in an airplane too, somewhere over Ohio, by now, I estimate, flying to a regional meeting, the first of the fall season, in Chicago. The fracturing of my little family, one-half north to Connecticut, one-quarter west to Illinois, and one-quarter south to Georgia is somehow both wondrous and awful—wondrous in its ease and awful in its implications. Families dispatched at will can perhaps be dispensed with at will.

The plane is dipping now for descent into Savannah. In a moment we will be meeting for the fourth time since it started. From Palm Beach in January to Savannah in September. Space age, mobile America, future shock. I am part of you now.

I wonder as I gather my things where he will go when he quits Jonas, and where we will go when I quit Jonas. But when I think about it, I get my dizziness, the vertigo that makes me fear the fall ahead, and so I try not to think about it for very long.

He is there. Perfect stranger. Imperfect Petrarch, furtive behind a pillar when I walk out of the docking tunnel into the terminal building. He squeezes my arm in a friendly way and takes my bag, which I have carried with me on the plane so as not to keep him waiting.

There is a gay courtliness about him as he inquires about the flight and asks if I have any further luggage. I believe he wants it to look as if he is meeting a customer, or a sister-in-law from New York. We walk briskly to the car. The etiquette of adultery, it seems, calls for rapid movements in one's home town.

He takes me to a house near Beaufort in South Carolina, about twenty miles up the highway from Savannah, but in another world. The town we go to has one store and a part-time post office. The frame house off the road at the end of a long desolate driveway was made for trysting. A friend's place, he told me vaguely when I persisted earlier. But I *had* to persist. I *had* to leave a number with Vivian, in case Jonas needed to reach me.

It has four square rooms downstairs and four upstairs and screened porches on both stories, in the back. Shaded by palmetto palms and live oaks veiled in Spanish moss, the back porches give onto a long pale lawn that ends in a bluff. We are on the same plane or savannah on which the city stands, I imagine.

Below, a small interesting river winds murkily along. I hear the putt-putt of a motor boat somewhere around the bend. The water eddies muddily around the staggering dock that belongs to the house, and an old man wearing a gone straw hat fishes off the end of the dock. "The village idiot," says Ian contemptuously. "Don't let him pester you." I look at Ian.

We go back into the house. The living room is furnished with things that were long ago somebody's best. Threadbare Oriental rugs, washed-out linen slipcovers on the couches, a ruby red chair with a broken wing, faded crewel draperies on poles at the windows. Bulging bookcases and numerous lamps indicate that someone who reads has furnished it. I do not know who that someone is.

Upstairs, where all the floors are stained dark brown and left uncarpeted, we lie on a fourposter bed covered with a patchwork quilt and close our eyes. There are thin white muslin curtains at the windows. What is wrong?

The room is northeast and deeply shaded. A door a few feet from me leading to the screened sleeping porch is open, and a breeze passes over me and chills me. I shiver. Whose house is this?

"Are you cold?" He asks me without opening his eyes.

"Yes."

"Get undressed."

We undress quickly and without the pleasure of helping hands and slip under the quilt. His body warms me instantly. He is like hot milk. We make love instantly too, and with no mistakes. We know by now exactly what we want and how. When the tension is dissipated and I am curled in his arms at ease, he cries. He is really like the woman in so many ways. I hold him and comfort him with my mouth. "I'm sorry I was so cold when you got here," he says. "I worked all weekend in the trees, and I hate all the lies."

Trees? Lies?

He works for the Arbor Tree Company on the weekends. A piano salesman, a jazz pianist, a hairdresser, now a tree man. What else does he do that I have yet to learn? I imagine him rigged high up in an oak or a blighted elm judiciously selecting with his pruning hook what must go.

Finally, I ask. "Whose house is this?"

"A friend's, I told you."

"A friend of Becky's, too?"

He laughs. "Oh, no. She doesn't know this friend."

"Why not?"

"She wouldn't approve. And we wouldn't be here if she knew him, would we? Do you think you know all of Jonas's friends?" Yes. I do.

There is so much I don't know about Ian.

"Don't you wonder where I am this week?" he asks.

Yes, Ian. I do. "Where are you?"

"Northern Florida down the east coast to Miami, with a day on the beach for good behavior."

"And you don't like all the lies."

"No, I don't."

Neither do I. But for some reason, I like the lies to Becky even less than the lies to Jonas.

I think of the lies I have told to get here. The intricacies would make a stronger woman reel. Only Ian can make me reel. Only Ian can make me real. "It will soon be all over."

We stay in bed until dusk, close and warm, and I feel very precious again. A valued possession again.

Georgia is having a cool snap. He builds a fire, and we sit in front of it on the sofa, our feet propped on a coffee table strewn with magazines, drinking bourbon and water and eating things he has bought for us: sharp cheddar, big stuffed olives, filberts.

I no longer feel there is anything strange about this house or being here with him. I feel right at home. I am where I want to be: alone with him at peace in a house we can call our own, warm, drowsy, flushed from fire, drink, and love, anonymous, safe, married in our way.

We are happy. We make love on the couch. My body heaves and sighs like the sea coming gently from his kiss. We have forgotten to draw the curtains, but no one is out there. And what if they were.

I am perfectly happy. Why is he the only man in the world who can make me feel this way?

The stove is hard to manage, perhaps because I have had too much bourbon, but he knows its secrets and gets the curried lamb noisettes going while I wash lettuce at the sink.

The kitchen has a tin ceiling, painted green, and a sink that exposes its workings, and a chipped enamel table, and an ancient gas-fueled refrigerator. Hot water comes out of the faucets, but it is hot by dint of a hard-working tank in the corner with an ominous flame under it that whooshes on and pops out in an alarming way. I dread having it near me, dread having such a thing in the house. We eat in the dining room, man and wife, two candles between us, the shadows on the walls our guests. How many children do you have? the shadows inquire. We have five children between us. Between us. We have five children between us.

"What is between us, Ian?" the bourbon asks. It's an odd expression. Between us. Is there anything between us? "Love," he says. "We have so much love between us."

It's all mixed up. I don't remember what I meant. It's such an odd expression. Between us.

I am drunk. I go upstairs and throw up in the toilet. After I have washed my face and cleaned out my mouth I throw up again. I am not used to drinking.

When I am sure I am well I go downstairs, gingerly, and sit on the couch. The fire is a bar of orange and hisses at me. He comes in from clearing the table in this house he knows so well and sits across from me in the red chair. He stares into the dying fire.

We sit without speaking. There is so much to say, so little to say. I wonder idly if the boys cried for me tonight. And I wonder if Jonas tried to call me in Boston, even though I told him not to, because Vivian was getting tickets for the nights that I would be there. I wonder.

We turn out the lights, screen the fire, close the hall windows, and go upstairs, like husband and wife. And, like husband and wife, he goes straight to sleep, while I lie awake and listen to rain plonking on the porch roof and wind scratching between the fronds of the palms. This is what life with Ian will be like. Secrets. It occurs to me before I fall asleep that this is not my dream. My dream was to be . . . a big girl. My act of rebellion was to have made me so. But it has not. I am still flying under the colors of my men. I do not yet know how to *be* authentic, what it takes. Opting for Ian has not freed me. It has only disoriented me. I feel, I know I repeat, deranged by . . . the promises I have to break, the lies I have to tell, the decisions I have to make, the quandary it puts me in.

20

IT is Saturday morning. Jonas is kneeling on the gravel outside the barn, repairing the lawn-sweeper. He is getting a head start on the season.

In warm slacks and a heavy sweater and wearing gloves, I am sitting near him, reading, or feigning.

The boys are all over, zooming in and out of the barn, climbing the stepladder which Jonas has had out, perhaps for retrieving a ball or their boomerang from the barn roof, and playing tag, with my chair as home base.

They buffet me. Everything buffets me these days. I think of a page from a rare manuscript at the library, the buffeting of Christ. He is sitting blindfolded in a chair, and Pilate from the background supervises his tormentors, who hit and push him about the head.

I feel pestered, an odd word. Ian said, don't let him *pester* you.

I want them to go away so I can be by myself, by Ian.

"Go away," I say to them crossly. "Stop grabbing onto my chair. Go play somewhere else." They vanish with a whoop. Jonas looks at me. I look back. What's it to you, I feel like saying. You go away, too.

I am boiling inside today. Seething about something. I am not sure what.

"That man is in the barn upstairs again," says Teddy, suddenly reappearing. I note with interest his blooming cheeks and, behind him, Peter, whose nose is running.

"What man?" asks Jonas, straightening up. His nose is running too. He takes a handkerchief out of his back pocket and honks into it.

"That man who's going to make our dam. The one who came to see Mom at the beach."

"What man?" He turns to me, puzzled, stuffing the handkerchief away again.

"I don't know of any man." I am frozen to my chair. My voice comes out high, as if from another realm.

He drops his pair of pliers. Pair of pliers? Pare of plyers? Pear? Pair? Why is it a *pair* of pliers? He drops his pliers. And looks up at the windows of the barn apartment. "We'll see," he mutters. The bamboo shade at the window is slightly askew.

"Jonas!"

His red and black lumber jacket vanishes inside the wide barn doors back into the dark behind the cars where the stairs to the apartment are.

"Jonas! Come back!" I run after him trying to pull him back down the stairs. He strides on, hauling me after him as a bike drags a branch caught in its spokes.

The room is deserted. Teddy darts between our legs. "In there, Dad!" he shouts. Jonas strides to the wardrobe, opens it with a crash, and pulls Ian out.

"Ian! Watch *out!*"

Jonas flings me away from him as the bike's boy flings the branch. I fall unnoticed onto the couch. He has Ian by the collar. He is beating him. Right fist, left fist, smash

146

backward, backward across the room backward! "Watch out!"

There is a sickening crash, the sound of broken glass. Screams. Like hay Ian is pitched through the plate-glass window that was the opening to the loft when this place was a farm.

He is lying unconscious on the gravel below, bloody. So bloody I scream, and wake up.

He is there next to me, under the quilt, sleeping on his back. My heart is pounding. I am dizzy with fright and in a sweat. Ian, I moan.

I climb on top of him. He stirs and kisses my face without really waking. Dry mouth of perfect shape. I love you, Ian. I *love* you. Do you hear?

He strokes my hips briefly through my thin gown. "Go back to sleep now," he mutters, rolling me off him. He turns over and is soon fast asleep again himself. I lie awake, thinking about my dream. Do I *want* Jonas to know?

21

THE rain stops toward morning and the eastern sky begins to brighten. What are we going to do all day? All our lives?

I am depressed about lives. So many lives. I fall asleep for a few hours to forget them.

When I wake it is raining again and there is a dent in the pillow where his head was. It is cold to my touch.

But then I hear him in the kitchen, cleaning up from last night, making breakfast.

He has started up last night's fire again from the embers to take the chill off the house. We carry our coffee in there and sit in front of it, on the couch, in our bathrobes. How strange for me to be here, after all.

"I have to go to Charleston this morning," he says. "For an interview."

Every now and then a raindrop falls down the chimney flue and sizzles out in the fire. I will never get used to his secretiveness.

"Oh?"

He names a competitor. His eyes have a strange light

in them. "They're looking for a regional manager for their southwest territory."

So far from home.

He reads my face. "Didn't you say you'd follow me anywhere?"

"Yes," I say in a high-pitched, formal voice, spoken into the coffee mug. I feel now as if I've burned my bridges. There is nothing to *do* but follow him. "I hope I can get the boys."

"Look," he says briskly. "I'll be back early. Before four. We'll have some of the afternoon left. Eat early. Smoke a joint tonight. O.K.?"

I nod. The bridge of my nose feels pinched as if something is in there gnawing at it under the skin, and I have the fluttering again in the little space in the center of my forehead.

"I've got some good stuff just for you," he says. "Want your maiden voyage to go just right."

I think of the Unicorn tapestries at the Cluny Museum in Paris. Capricorn thought she had Unicorn. But the mystical beast is a symbol of purity, and I noticed how he sprinkled Accent on the lamb chops last night.

Before he leaves, in a gray glen-plaid suit and a wide blue tie, very natty, I ask him to pump up the tires of the bike in the garage. And draw me a map. He tells me to be sure to visit the Antebellum houses in Beaufort and to note the buildings made of tabby—crushed oyster shells—along the wharf. (Natural, naturally; also indigenous.)

He does the tires, but forgets the map.

I stop at the store on the road and ask the way to Beaufort. They look at me as if they know who I am and where I am staying and with whom, and unsmilingly indicate the way.

I buy a map in a gift shop in Beaufort. There is also an arsenal here and a national cemetery. I wonder how closely they are related. A Marine Corps facility is nearby too. And piney woods. The old and the new. I want something natural too. And not Beaufort tabby. I am only in this cute town for half an hour when I want to get out of it.

I turn off the white cement highway into the woods. Thick, silent, fragrant, green, sun-touched, orderly, bisected by an easy-to-take flat dirt road, the pine woods are good. I pedal slowly in peace and quiet down the long road, my head up to catch the sweet pine smell in my face and the warmth of the weak sun through the parting clouds. The woods have nothing to do with life out on the highway. Nothing to do with Ian.

And, for the time being, anyway, I do not want anything to do with Ian, because I see that I am going to be an appendage to his life, too, a little blind worm of a vermiform appendix that follows him everywhere, and this nasties me, this realization. The vermiform appendix, my biology coming back to me in a burst of insight, is thought to be in the process of gradual obliteration in the human species. If it would *do* something it might be allowed to stay, but it doesn't. It just hangs there, short on blood. And as for doing something, I can imagine that, in the great Southwest, curators of medieval and Renaissance manuscripts have little need to do much of anything.

Although these pleasant pine woods have nothing to do with Ian, Ian has something to do with them. And that I pedal right into without any warning.

The grunting yellow bulldozers grinding into reverse, charging forward to attack the enemy, the pine woods.

On my right is a red sea of tree stumps, acres and acres of them, roots upended grotesquely in the air, dotting the clayey field like some loathsome acne. A huge fire at the other end of what presumably will be a shopping center, long football fields away, is being fueled with pine trees by men in blue jackets. When I get near them I read Arbor Tree Demolition Company on the backs of their jackets. A dense pungent pine smoke blackens the air. Arbor Tree *Demolition* Company. He left that part out. What else has he left out?

"What am I supposed to do?" he whines. "I've got a wife and three kids to support, and now you."

"You don't have to do anything for *me*."

"You don't have to do anything for *me*," he mimics. "What do you think I'm doing for you already?"

Oh.

That's how it is.

I put it right out of my mind.

I close my eyes and grin. The marijuana is taking hold of us, I guess. I rather like it.

He gets up and starts to dance by himself around the dining room table. La la la *la* la *la* la *la*. A waltz. He circles around and around, holding a partner with one hand, a long skirt with the other, his shadow on the wall an elegant impersonation dipping and swaying to his lead.

The music on the record player does not seem to be a waltz at all to me, but tinny Oriental music with tinkling bells and an insistent beat of drums I did not notice before. I put my head down on the dining room table and float away into pleasant euphoria with a grinny grin grin. I feel lovely and peaceful and very happy. Very happy. Everything is going to work out.

When it has passed away and we are yawning and still grinning we make lovely languid love and everything *is* all right again. He tells me Becky won't do it. I'll do anything, I murmur. Show me what to do.

22

YOU'RE the third one he's had here," says the old man in the straw hat. "He won't leave his wife for you nor nobody."

I look steadfastly at the crabs heaving and writhing in his basket.

He peers at me from under the brim of his hat, calculating. "The others were dark-haired," he says, "but both of 'em was married."

I walk quickly away, back to the house under the Spanish moss and the palmetto palms. Woodsmoke in the air faintly suggests our last night's fire. The dizziness is in my head.

Never again Georgia.

23

"YOU never answered my question that time," I say in the car on the way to the airport.

"What time?" He bears down on the highway.

"In the hotel. The first time I came to Savannah."

"What question?"

How would he remember that? "It doesn't matter." I look out the window on my side at the tracts of pine flying past. There are plenty of woods left. I guess it doesn't matter. Was there somebody else the other times? I naïvely wanted to know. It was all based, after all, on my thinking I was unique, wasn't it, Ian? Your first, your last.

Well, things are not always what they seem. He was right about that in Palm Beach.

He kisses me good-bye in the passengers' lounge. "Don't wait," I say.

"I'll be in touch," he says. "As soon as I hear about the job." He walks away, turning once to wave and blow a kiss.

24

I T is October now. The leaves are all falling at once today, dripping down incessantly with the same crunchy sound that gypsy moth larvae make when they are all eating a whole woods at once and letting it all out at once at the other end. Except that this rain is pretty. It is sad, though, too.

I am feeling very well. The fluttering in the space behind my forehead is gone, and I am going to be fine. All I needed, really, was time, a little time to think it all over, to unknot the knots inside my skull, to get used to my new remodeled twentieth-century self.

I'm glad I'm feeling this way, so optimistic, and in time too to appreciate the fall colors—the last bit of them before the woods around turn sere. I stayed in the house for nearly a month, thinking things over. Everyone was very concerned about me.

My friends have all been so good, sending me things to amuse myself. Jonas looked at everything I got and gently took some things away—a jigsaw puzzle from Jo-Anne with five hundred pieces that were supposed to make a picture of Joe Namath when they were all fit together. I guess he thought it would tax me.

Nervous breakdowns are loud and noisy and embarrassing, throwing things or getting undressed in public or urinating in a potted plant at a party. So I didn't have one. It wouldn't be me at all to act like that, even under conditions of the utmost stress, which they were, for me, learning that Ian wasn't—or, rather, was—what I thought he was. I did love you, Ian. I think I *would* have followed you anywhere.

My little mental eruption was quiet and restrained and dignified, like me. It didn't attract any attention at all, outside of my family, and they only noticed because I didn't get up to make breakfast one morning. When I still hadn't gotten up two days later, Jonas called the doctor, he who had so deftly tied my tubes a season back. He came right over even though it was a Sunday. He was wearing his tennis whites.

Postoperative depression, he said, as he picked up a perfume atomizer from the dresser and sniffed at it. Delayed. Acute. Needs to get away. A nice rest. Know a good place.

I reared up in my bed and said, I'm not going anywhere. I'm staying right here. I just want to be left alone for a while.

They walked about in my bedroom. Two men, saying things to each other with their eyes that I couldn't hear.

I didn't even want to hear. They'll never know what happened. Let them think they do. I just need to be by myself for a while. It's not the easiest thing, being deceived. Or deceiving either. Deceive not; grieve not.

Now I know what it was I was trying to think of last summer on Long Island—the thing that had to do with

Ian. It was how he was bringing me up-to-date, putting me in tune with the times. But I had a horror of the times, Ian. I didn't want that.

I lie on the chaise on the back lawn wrapped in a blanket and look at the rain of leaves and think over all the modern things I've done this year because of him:

Listened to ABC
Bought rock records
Wore eye makeup
Went without a bra
Had my ears pierced
Drove the car fast with the radio on
Committed adultery
Got myself sterilized
Smoked pot
and Learned that things are not always what they seem.

I didn't want to be *renovated*, Ian; I just wanted to live happily ever after with you. But thanks just the same. It's not as bad as I thought it would be, joining the twentieth century. And, really, it was about time I did anyway, about time I gave up my medieval chain-of-being outlook, about time I realized we are not all arranged in a perfect Thomistic hierarchy, our positions fixed and immutable. Yes, it was about time I made the great leap forward to grasp the tricky notion that we are our own choices. Thank you for that, Ian, for being the lever (lover) that I used to put me over the top of that steep idea.

Nothing has changed at home, except the season. Oh, yes. Jonas called the mason to come back and take down the walls of my garden. Of all things, Jonas *is* what he seems. No reality gap *there* at all. But I spoke sharply, in italics, and the walls stayed. Even though Ian was wrong about it, the garden in Chelsea. It isn't clear at all that it was or wasn't walled. I had the library send the book over again. That's how I know. So much for literary compatibility.

Jonas doesn't know anything, but his wanting the walls down tells me that something inside him knows something but doesn't know what it is it knows. Anyway, he was telling me that such little acts of rebellion as laying brick walls without his permission are behind us from now on. That's all right with me. I've performed the act, the existential act of rebellion that was needed, and it did its work. I won't be needing to build gardens again for perfect strangers. Ian, how *could* you treat me like that, play me so false? You made a fool of me. And I thought you were so good. But you made something else out of me, too, and thanks for that, dear one who loved me in his way.

Enna Jetticks is back to mind the boys. But she's supposed to be keeping an eye on me, too, without my being supposed to know it. And my friends, they drop in one at a time, one or two every day. I wouldn't be surprised if they had a duty chart worked out. If you do my car pool today, I'll do Lily for you tomorrow. I don't care.

They all point out, as if I'd never thought of it, that I didn't want another baby anyway. I agree with them, and although it is true, of course, they don't really believe me. "It was just the shock of it," I say. "I needed a rest afterward."

"Maybe it's reversible," they all suggest.

"But I don't *want* to reverse anything. I'm glad I did it, glad it's all over. I feel much freer now. And I still look the same, don't I?" I enjoy talking to them on two levels like that.

I called Mr. D'Allessandro and asked him to recommend

me for a job I heard about. There's an opening in January in Stamford for a docent. Mornings. It's not a copout. It's my choice. It's what's possible right here and now. I didn't say it had to be forever.

On top of it all, I'm glad I was able to handle it, my confrontation with reality, without putting anyone to too much trouble. And proud, too. I weathered the storm all alone. Nobody knows what happened. And nobody ever will. That's *my* secret, and in the end my strength.

And, Ian, thanks for the good news, that things are not always what they seem; that's one small lesson I learned from you, even though in one way you've disproved it, too. After all, you appeared to be a young husband upward bound in his career, and that's just what you turned out to be, isn't it?

On the other hand, Ian, I am not what you, wherever you are now, may think *I* seem to be: defeated and deceived, an appendage still. No, Ian, I am no longer the little-girl wife, uncoping with impunity. I have coped. I shall cope. I can do what I set my mind to do. I am not deceived. I am finally not. After it all, I am Lily, tall, decorous, dignified, and undeceived.

I am indomitable. That's what I learned. Do you hear that, Ian?